...rt

...04)

...ard, which

... in the trilogy, *The Time We Have Taken*, wo... in 2008. Steven Carroll lives in Melbourne with his partner and son.

Praise for *The Art of the Engine Driver*

'An exquisitely crafted journey of Australian suburban life . . . fresh and irresistible.'

Miles Franklin Literary Award Judges, 2002

'Deceptively simple, this novel has a quiet force.'

Sydney Morning Herald

'From the first lines of this very beautiful novel by Steven Carroll, an indefinable charm is at work.'

Le Monde

'A little masterpiece.'

Hessische Allgemeine

'The Art of the Engine Driver is a stunning work of masterful story-telling and sparing, assured prose.'

Télérama

'A brilliant novel.'

Brigitte

The Art of the Engine Driver

Steven Carroll

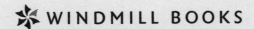

WINDMILL BOOKS

Published by Windmill Books 2010

2 4 6 8 10 9 7 5 3 1

Copyright © Steven Carroll 2001

First published in Australia in 2001 by HarperCollins*Publishers*

Windmill Books
The Random House Group Limited
20 Vauxhall Bridge Road, London SW1V 2SA

Addresses for companies within The Random House Group Limited can be
found at: www.randomhouse.co.uk/offices.htm

The Random House Group Limited Reg. No. 954009

www.rbooks.co.uk

A CIP catalogue record for this book
is available from the British Library

ISBN 9780099537274

The Random House Group Limited supports The Forest Stewardship
Council (FSC), the leading international forest certification organisation. All
our titles that are printed on Greenpeace approved FSC certified paper carry
the FSC logo. Our paper procurement policy can be found at:
www.rbooks.co.uk/environment

FT
Pbk

Printed and bound in Great Britain by
Cox & Wyman, Reading, RG1 8EX

contents

Part Two
Saturday Night

Epilogue
Sunday Morning

Prologue

Saturday Evening

I.

Group Portrait

They're walking down the old street again, Rita, Vic, and the boy, Michael. It's summer, a warm breezy evening, and they are walking under a cloudless peach sky, ripe and glowing. The sun is low and their shadows almost stretch back to the family house at the golf course end of the street.

They've reached that point in their walk, the halfway mark, where the houses and yards suddenly taper off into Scotch thistle and open, swaying grass. The sun has nearly dropped to earth and the three of them have stopped, staring out across the blades of whispering grass and thistle, across to the flour mills and railway lines, as if expecting a low, distant thud.

Vic's white, open-necked shirt is more in keeping with the late 1940s than the late 1950s. But Rita's dress, yellow and black, with bright flowers and one dark bold strap, is a garment of its times. For this suburb, a garment ahead of its times. Her hair is dyed, with a faint suggestion of red, and bounces occasionally about her neck as she walks. Michael is wearing his best shirt. Short sleeves, short pants. Rita turned thirty-three last autumn, Vic is forty, Michael is twelve. There they are, still as a photograph, listening for the distant thud of the sun as it prepares to drop from the sky, out there, somewhere beyond the railway lines and the flour mills.

But, behind the mills, the sun stays on a little longer than usual, the vacant paddock glowing white and gold beyond its allotted time and, for a moment, everything promises to go on forever; sunsets, afternoons, Saturday nights, marriages, and lives. No fates to be met because nobody is going anywhere. No turning earth beneath the dirt footpath, no movement in the sky. No setting of the sun. No waning of the moon.

The family moves on, towards the Englishman's house at the bottom of the street − where an engagement party is to be held. George Bedser's daughter, Patsy, is getting engaged and the whole street has been invited. All around the recreation of the day is now complete, the tennis courts, the golf course and the cricket grounds are empty. The stumps have been drawn, the nets, rackets and clubs put away. The players have gone home and are dressed for Saturday night.

Now, slowly, one after the other, the front doors and front gates of the street are opening out onto their lawns, footpaths and nature strips, as all the families, like a well rehearsed ensemble, step onto the dusty dirt road and form a modest procession, trailing perfume, aftershave and the faint whiff of mothballs.

As the stars take their places, the long, white tail of a comet becomes visible. By now everybody is used to the sight of this comet burning its way through space. At first the street had gazed up to the sky in wonder. But it wasn't long before everybody forgot to look up and the wonder disappeared. For the comet had made slow progress across the suburb all summer.

The three of them pause by the swaying grass of the vacant land and Rita looks up and squints.

'It's like a tablet.' She's laughing, pleased with herself.

The whole family looks up and nods. So it is. Like a tablet dissolving in a vast, liquid sky. Although the comet had made slow progress, and even though it never appeared to be moving at all, everybody was assured that it was moving all right. The more it moved, the more it dissolved. And, sooner more likely than later, somebody would casually look up to the sky on their evening walk back from the station and find it gone.

At that moment Rita is staring at Vic, and Michael is now watching her. Rita looks puzzled, as if silently asking the question of Vic, 'Who are you?' She knows and she doesn't know. She has known him for years and she'll never know him. He's an engine driver. He's funny, a bit of a poet, a dag. But he drinks too much. It's all that life he's got in him. Doesn't know when to stop. And he should because he's a lousy drunk. But she knew that before she married him.

Rita works with motors too. She demonstrates washing machines to buyers. From the heavy-duty factory machines to small domestic tubs. She's often in the country for a week or more, talking into a microphone to hundreds of housewives at a time in large country stores. She complains about the travel. He complains about the engines, wants to be done with them, but she knows he'd be washed up without them.

The suburb is new, built around an old farming township. The bluestone farmhouses still control the few vantage points of the low, broad valley on which the community sits, but the new lines of the suburb are taking shape. Streets and salubriously named dirt avenues have been carved out of the paddocks and houses have begun to appear; red roofs, white weatherboards and instant gardens, sprouting like fold-out models. Cattle refuse to accept the newly drawn suburban boundaries and graze where they always have, even if it is now somebody's front yard, and even if it means a diet of yellow roses instead of clover.

The main street – an old wheat road that leads to the mills, and then, by rail, to the Melbourne warehouses only nine miles away – contains two imposing, double-storey shops, all that remain of the 1880s land boom, when big plans had been made for the area. But the boom never happened as the estate agents had promised, and the shops became dusty and run down, selling Indian Root pills, shovels, picks, fence wire, fly powder, starch, shirt collars, yeast tablets, cornflour, broken biscuits, and whatever else would keep them going.

For the next seventy years nothing much changed. After the war a factory was built on cheap land near the railway station, and the owner built himself a large house on expansive grounds not far away. And now every day, over dirt roads, he travels to and from his factory in a chauffeur-driven Bentley. Slowly, so that the dark figure in the back, like royalty that has only recently paid off his title, can survey the flat expanse of his domain with ease. Slowly, so that the suspension of the Bentley won't be damaged by the potholes in the street. Slowly, so that everybody he passes on the footpaths and corners will pause, staring at the shining black majesty of the Bentley as it makes its daily pilgrimage from mansion to factory to mansion.

With the factory came workers, new houses, new shops. And with the success of one factory, came another. And another. Estate agents, the eager grandsons, returned to create the land boom their grandparents had anticipated seventy years before and promised all their young buyers exactly the same again. A district of dignified houses, profuse gardens and shaded avenues. Everybody looking good in this Toorak of the north. And all for a hundred quid a block.

All around, a suburb is being born. But it won't be the suburb the agents guaranteed. Like all booms it will soon turn into a rush, a land grab, and, within a few years, cheap workers' homes will be thrown up by builders who are always starting another house even as they are finishing the one they're on. The city is spilling out across the coastal plain and time will eventually catch up with the area.

As Vic, Rita and Michael make their way down to the Englishman's house that time is still travelling towards them, part of a future not yet fully formed, and the community is still hovering between town and country.

Before them the road dips into a slight hollow and, to their left across the open paddocks, the red-brick buildings, the cream wooden shelter sheds and the asphalt playgrounds of the school are visible through the tall pines and peppercorns. The morning before, Michael and all the assembled students of the school had marched into their classrooms, two by two, with recorded brass music in their ears. A few moments before, Michael had watched from the shade of the shelter shed as three boys from the sixth grade approached three of their classmates. These three boys had been selected to have the shit beaten out of them by the Camp Pell kids. They had paired off, one side to be beaten, the other to do the beating, when the bell went. The school assembled, the brass music began, the six boys dropped their arms, joined the assembly and soon after entered the cool, chalky quiet of the classrooms. Now, the quadrangle is empty, and only a slight breeze ruffles the pines.

Even as it does, in the back yard of a house in the next street, one of the boys who had been selected for a beating is standing with his mother on the dirt patch that will become their lawn. The mother is teaching the boy how to box. She is teaching him how to raise his arms and protect himself. How to block the blows. How to watch, how to wait and when to strike. They are circling each other, mother and son, on the dirt patch that will become their lawn, the mother slapping the boy about the ears every time he drops his arms, hardening the boy's heart, so that he won't whimper, and he won't cry, and he won't be hurt when she's not there.

And so, oblivious of the sky, unaware of anything special in its colour, the mother and son continue circling each other well into the night, while out on the dirt footpath of the next street up, Vic, Rita and Michael are standing by the long swaying grass of the vacant paddock. Before them, in the hollow at the end of the street, the lights of the Englishman's house are already on, its windows crisp, distant squares of pale yellow.

Years later, Michael will dream of this evening. It will be vivid. He will go back to the suburb in dreams, stand on the street and see them all again as they are this night, walking down to the Englishman's house under the last of the summer sky. He will see the lines across Vic's wide forehead, the hair parted down the middle, the dark waves brushed to the sides. He will see the sparkle in Rita's eyes, the bounce of her hair and note the glitter of her seashell earrings. He will observe himself, wearing the good white shirt with the button-down collar that he loved so much but had forgotten all about until his dream took him back to the old street. They will all be there before him again, clear, solid, alive.

But even with hindsight, even in dreams, he will still comb through the wreckage of this night in search of another ending, one that will cheat fate and shift the course of their lives. But it won't be there, and what was always going to happen, will happen, again and again and again.

At the moment, however, Vic, Rita and Michael are standing perfectly still under a miraculously peach-coloured sky. All around them, the front doors of the houses are open to let the breeze through. Venetian blinds flutter briefly, lounge-room curtains lift like billowed sails, then settle again. Mrs Miller calls to her husband for her new locket, the telephone in Mr Van Rijn's study rings, Bruchner's dog yelps at an unapologetic black cat perched on the back fence, Mr Malek steps uncertainly up to his front gate, Evie Doyle begins washing another stack of dishes in the golf course kitchen and Patsy Bedser switches on the new hi-fi in the lounge room before the guests arrive.

In that clear summer air it is possible to see into the hallways, the rooms and back yards; possible to hear the loud, the low and the murmured voices, both inside the houses and out on the street.

Part One

Saturday Evening

2.

The Art of Engine Driving

There is a train out there somewhere. Vic lights a cigarette, drops the match then turns his head to one side, facing Rita, so as to hear it better. With his ears to the west, and his eyes on the still figure of his wife lingering by the long grass of the paddock, he listens to the train.

He knows it's a goods. And, by the time of the evening, he can judge where it's come from, the stops it's made on the way. He knows how full it is from the thud of the wheels hitting the rail joints just as he knows the class of the engine from the sound of its motor. And when he's put all this information together he might even be able to tell you who the driver is. For he knows their styles, most of them, the best of them, the artists. He knows their characteristics, their defining touches, the signatures that they leave on the rails, there to be read by those who know how, as clearly as a painter's on a canvas.

Vic can visualise the scene in the cabin. The gauges are all lit up before him in the night. The speed, the steam, the air pressure. All there before him, but he never reads them. Driving is a gift. Physical. Something you've either got or you haven't. Some drivers watch the needles bobbing about in front of them all night, the needles, the gauges and the numbers. They drive by the book, but he threw the book away the first night he got in the cabin and sat in the driver's seat.

You can stick your numbers and gauges. I don't trust them. I never have and I never will. Oh, you can drive by the book, take the curves and the descents at regulation speed and you'll arrive on time and everybody will call you a good driver. But a great driver drives with his fingertips and his arms, his shoulders, his stomach, the back of his neck, his intestines, his entrails and toes. You don't need gauges, your body's full of them. It's telling you what you need to know, all the time. But only a few listen. And that's the difference between a good driver and a great one. The great drivers listen.

When I'm out there in the night, in the rainy hills and the soaked cuttings and there's another train coming towards me, its headlights making a yellow path through the forest and clouds, I know within seconds if I'm watching a great driver. By the speed, the controlled daring, or the way a driver prepares for a sudden, clean descent. The great drivers will leave their individual stamp all over the move. They won't be reading gauges, they'll be listening to their bodies and listening to the engine. And all the time, all through the journey, as they scatter the cattle and the low mist before them, the boast will be, and the boast will be true, that the full metal mug of tea sitting beside the driver's seat was never once disturbed.

Driving begins with shaving, once, then twice. A good sharp razor and lather. You can't drive without a clean face.

When you come to the curves and bends, lean out of the window and turn your face to the wind, and the air on your cheek will tell you all you need to know. It will tell you the speed of the engine more accurately than any instrument. If it's too fast or too slow. Then look down to the sleepers flying past beneath you and pay attention to what your eyes and the clean-shaven side of your face tell you.

There are times, coming down through the mountains with a trainload of ballast behind me, when I forget the instrument panel altogether, forget the speed regulation notices by the side of the rails along the way, and take all the winding curves that lead down into a waiting station by feel alone. The trees are rushing by in the night, the train's creaking and groaning behind me as the weight shifts from side to side, and I can feel the wind on one cheek and the glow of the furnace on the other, as the forest parts and the low clouds get out of the way. The speed regulation signs go by so fast I couldn't read them if I wanted to. Then, when we hit the incline I always knew was there – because the first thing you do in this game is learn your roads and gradients by heart – the engine hums up the hill and takes it in one mighty wallop, and we take that last ride down onto the plain, using the wide, sweeping curve of the rails to slow the train. And by the time we hit the flat that leads into the station we're back to regulation speed again. No one knows how I do it, and I'm not telling. That's my business. All I can say is it's like dancing. You never doubted that your feet would take you where you wanted them to be. That's driving too. And you don't do it by following the book. I know the guard's been hanging onto his seat back there in the van, and the stationmaster's slowly shaking his head in the light of his lamp as we ease into the platform because he heard us roaring down through the hills like we were going to take the whole station with us.

From there on it's flat land and level track. In a few hours the sky starts to lighten, yellow and rose, and we're driving into the best part of the day. The part nobody sees. The city laid out before us. Wide and flat. Street after street, front yard after front yard. In the distance I'll see my own suburb, picture my house, my family asleep inside. I'll sleep through the day, then rise in the afternoon, wash and shave, fill my bag with tea and tinned stew, tobacco, cakes of yellow soap and swabs. All in readiness for the night again; for the hills, the curves, the cutting, and the stations that will stay lit up because they know we're out there.

3.

Pausing by the Paddock

Rita fixes the comet with her eyes. She squints into the sky trying to calculate the point at which the comet will become indistinguishable from the stars themselves or disappear altogether. Then the distant sound of a goods train, rattling down into the city, drags her away from the sky. Vic is lighting a cigarette on the edge of the paddock. The glow of the match is almost the colour of the sky. The faint, disappearing rattle of the engine fading in her ears, while she concentrates on the still, silent, glow of the match.

She hears the engine in another time, the hiss of the brakes. The crunch of the gravel beneath her feet. A suitcase beside her. Sees the grey country sky and the slate on the roof of the station, shiny like glass. She hears the carriage doors closing behind her and the platform whistle as the train leaves.

He stood there in front of me in his work clothes, not saying anything. No, of course not. We both just stood there on the platform, neither of us saying a word. Already, we'd started that childish game of who'd be the first to speak, the first to break. I was tired of it. I wanted to get on the train again and go back to my real home, back in the city, but the train had gone.

The platform was empty. Nobody hangs around platforms, but we did. It must have been two, three or five minutes. It's hard to say.

'How have you been?'

'Good.'

That's all. He looked away as he said it, across the rails to the shunted carriages and guard's vans. Good. Nothing more than that. It had been two weeks since I left. Two weeks since we'd spoken.

I wasn't coming back. Wasn't even considering it. Not till he'd promised this, pledged to do that. Not till he'd smartened his act up. Not till he'd given up the grog and the useless mates he drank with that only dragged him down.

So I left and went back to mama's. We'd been married less than a year. Poor mama. Watching over me all the time, and talking to me all the time, just to make me feel better. But she didn't. It was either too much or nothing at all. No talk or so much it may as well be nothing. For the previous two weeks I'd been sitting in my old room, sleeping in my old room and waking in my old room like nothing had changed.

Every day I heard my mama in the yard. I heard the creak of the clothesline, the flap of the shirts in the wind, bright in the morning sun. My old things were still in the room. Movie magazines. Everywhere, movie magazines. I'd forgotten how many there were. The old wardrobe, with all the old dresses. But none of it was mine any more and I kept on just wishing he'd write or call. After the first week I knew he was waiting for me to break and phone first.

The country seemed like a good idea after we married. Get away from everybody. From the pubs, from the boozers. It's no way to start a marriage, with that lot hanging around. A clean sweep, he said. And so off we went. At first I didn't care where we were. All we could find was a half house in the town behind a fruit shop. I didn't care. There was a yard, a vegetable patch, a fruit tree. For a while it worked. But there's pubs and boozers everywhere.

I smell the pubs and the stale beer. Right here, beside this paddock. Beside the swaying grass and the schoolyard pines, I smell them all. Stale and sickly. I smell them as clearly as I heard the crunch of the gravel under my feet that evening on the platform. He carried my bag and we walked up the platform to the ticket collector who'd been waiting all that time.

I'd been away two weeks and if I hadn't phoned he never would have written and I would have still been sitting back in my old room listening to mama. The ticket collector smiled and we walked down the asphalt path to the street. Without turning, he told me that he'd cooked dinner.

It was late in the afternoon and getting dark and the shops in the street were lit up. It was only then I noticed he was wearing his good shoes under his overalls. That they'd been cleaned and shined, the way only black can shine. We moved along under the verandahs. The shops were shutting but I could smell the bakery and we kept it open to buy cake. We were quiet and calm. Nobody was weeping. Nobody was shouting or sighing. And, without a word being said, it was clear that nobody was promising anything they couldn't keep to.

And soon I was in that tiny room again at the back of the fruit shop. The one we cooked in, and ate in, and sat in for almost a year before I left. The radio was on and he was talking about work. About engines. My bag was in the bedroom, still packed.

It was cold that first night back, country cold, but somehow that room felt good. It had no right to, but it did. And the smell of the stew as he's dished it up. Of all the meals I've eaten over all the years, I only remember a few. But I remember that one. The steam off the plate, the peas and the salty smell of the gravy, like it's under my nose now. And I shouldn't have felt hungry, but I was ravenous. Like I could have eaten the whole pot. I didn't know what had come over me, as soon as my bowl was finished I wanted it filled again. And he was laughing all the time, saying tuck in girl, you haven't eaten all day. I had. I knew I had, but that didn't stop me.

And when I'd finished the third bowl, when I'd put the plate back on the table and licked the last of the gravy from the spoon. When I'd pushed the plate away after eating enough for two people and I was staring at the smoke rising from his fingers, with the taste of the stewed meat on my lips, on my breath, and the juices of the stew flowing through my veins and my skin tingling all over, then, I knew why I'd come back.

Afterwards, he washed the dishes. You sit down, he said, and turned back to the sink, still in his good shoes. Mind you, he hadn't said a word about the previous two weeks. It was like I'd been on a holiday, or never been away at all. And I was the one who wasn't coming back. I swore I wasn't coming back, but I did. And that night I discovered why.

He whistled along to some song on the radio and it was a good sound. After the meal it was pleasant on the ears, so pleasant I could almost have forgotten I'd been away. Then there was the cool smell of the bedroom. My bag was by the chest of drawers and I put my clothes away. Back into the same drawers I'd taken them out of two weeks before.

The sheets of the bed were white and cold but I knew they'd soon warm up. He was in the kitchen, still whistling. Every now and then the sounds of the radio drifted up from the back of the house along the hallway. My toothbrush was in a glass by the bowl in the bathroom, all ready for the morning, and all the mornings and all the days after that. Outside, a cloud was swept from the sky and a big, white moon pressed its face up against the window.

Rita watches as the match flares and dies. Vic drops it at his feet on the footpath then turns to her, as if to say what's keeping you. Rita's not moving. She's standing by the edge of the paddock in a dress that is just a bit too good for this street and the faint taste of that meal still on her lips.

4.

Pausing by the Paddock

Michael stares at the stationary figures of his mother and father; his mother looking quizzically at his father, his father still with his ears turned towards the railway line, listening to the train as it passes. He's here but he's not here, Michael thinks. The sun is low and the three of them stand bright in the last of that Saturday night sun.

Just as the train fades, the ripe bells of St Matthews swell in the close air, two notes slowly following each other at even intervals. One overlapping, then succeeding the other, before being succeeded itself. It is a small wooden church with a weatherboard belfry and stands on the corner of the main road, back towards the railway line. It is near and the bells are clear. To Michael these bells always called from another time, even another country. And they always sounded like the end of something, but he could never tell what.

His parents are the length of a cricket pitch apart, and Michael, in the middle, can observe them freely, for they seem to have forgotten all about him. They could be meeting for the first time. They could be strangers and he has the sudden, uneasy feeling that he doesn't really know who these people are. When they stand like this, separate, silent, in their own worlds like statues on museum lawns, he is seeing something of who they were before he came along.

The previous winter, after school one evening, when his father was at night shift and his mother was at work and he was alone in the house, he took the shopping trolley and wheeled it along the dirt path that led to the station. By five it was already dark and he stood outside the ticket collector's gate and watched the yellow lights of the train as it pulled into the platform. In the waiting room some of the passengers took their good work shoes off and changed into their old shoes, for the waiting room was lined with the old, dirty shoes that everybody used for the muddy walk back from the station. When the passengers strode out onto the asphalt path keen for home, he looked for his mother. But the last of them came and went and she wasn't there. He stood in his cardigan, hunched over the shopper, and waited for the next train.

When it arrived and its red doors swung open he watched the crowd once more heading towards the waiting room for their shoes, then on to the ticket collector's gate.

She didn't see him at first. Nor did he immediately recognise her. She looked different. What she is, he guessed, during the day when she's working. He stood near the ticket gate, with the red-brick Post Office behind him, watching the people in their hats and coats, carrying their bags and clutching their evening newspapers, and wondering if he should be there at all, the only child at the station. But then she saw him and smiled and he knew it was all right. She put her bag in the trolley and together they took the asphalt path down to the shops.

In the butcher's shop he stood back against the wall, playing with the sawdust at his feet while his mother talked to the butcher. They laughed and talked like old friends and once again Michael felt like he shouldn't be there. When his mother took the chops and the mince, the butcher called her by her name, Rita, as he waved goodbye and Michael connected that name with his mother as if learning it all over again.

When she closed the vinyl lid of the shopper, she smiled and told him what a good idea it was to bring the shopping trolley to the station, and they walked back along the dirt path, Michael pushing the trolley, his mother nodding in the dark street to his comments, saying yes or no to his questions. Sometimes she was silent. During those silences Michael occasionally looked up from the trolley at her, making out her features in the dark, the hair, cut and combed like an actress, the make-up, the lipstick red in the shadows. And even though he thought she might turn at any moment and catch him staring, she didn't. She was looking ahead, along the street, and he wanted to know what she was thinking.

It is then that Rita calls out to Vic, across that imaginary cricket pitch that divides them, and tells him to wait. They should all walk to the party together, she says. Like a family, she adds. And so Vic waits as Rita joins him. As soon as she does Michael begins his run, slowly accelerating, his shoulders level, his paces even as he nears his delivery stride. When he hits the point of delivery Vic and Rita step back quickly to make way as Michael bowls an imaginary cricket ball into the twilight like the great Lindwall. Michael is cricket mad. The fence at the back of their house, against which he bowls every day, bears the marks of his madness. Michael stops and stares into the distance following the path of the invisible ball. He then turns back to his parents and they continue their walk down the dirt footpath to the Englishman's house at the bottom of the street.

5.

Studying Ray Lindwall

The wooden fence at the back of the yard is already splintered and broken above where three white lines representing stumps have been painted. Every day Michael bowls against the fence and the fence is slowly falling apart. He has been bowling at the fence all summer and now he can see through the opening onto the green lawn of next door's back yard.

From the moment he first saw the game played it was the fast bowler that caught his eye. Michael thinks of nothing else but fast bowling through the long school days, and dreams of fast bowling at night. Just one dream. And always the same. In this dream he bowls the perfect ball. He experiences its perfection from beginning to end. It is a delivery so perfect that it becomes known all over the suburb as the ball that Michael bowled. The scene is always the same. The red train at the local station is just pulling out from the platform, the mill cats are tumbling over each other in the Saturday-afternoon sun, a vase of flowers at the base of the war memorial bows to the footpath in the heat, the milk bar owner in the main street pours lemonade into a glass for a lime spider, while on the dusty schoolyard oval in the shade of the great pines, Michael bowls the perfect ball and everything stops. The train delays its departure. The milk bar owner turns from his lime spider. The mill cats look up from their games as word ripples through the suburb that Michael has bowled the perfect ball. And the witnesses, those who were there, will grow in number throughout the day and through the following weeks, till everyone will claim to have been there and witnessed the ball that young Michael bowled. And all will agree, from the moment the ball left the boy's hand, to the moment it lifted the off stump from the ground, that it was the perfect ball and that the boy had a gift for speed.

It is his ambition that one day he will live his dream. That one day he will feel the ball leave the tips of his thumb and fingers, know from the moment it does what is about to happen, and look up from his delivery stride to see the schoolyard crowd and everybody on the street that runs alongside the oval, pause in wonder as something of distracting perfection enters the everyday world of school bells and midday shopping. And even those who don't care for the game will nod to each other on the footpaths, acknowledging that it is an event.

But before that moment can be lived he will spend his days bowling against his back fence, until that part of the fence upon which the three stumps have been painted will shatter completely and a new set of stumps will need to be drawn in.

Every day Michael kneels on the lawn with a small house-painting brush in one hand and draws a white line across the grass. On the lawn there are always two opened books lying in the sun. The pages of one contain a series of eight photographs, a series of newsreel stills that show, frame by frame, the great Lindwall's action. Lindwall is shown approaching the crease. Michael sees the bowler gathering himself for the delivery stride. Lindwall hits the delivery stride, sliding through on the point of his right boot then transfers his weight to the front foot. The next frame is the boy's favourite. Lindwall's arm is high, his back is arched, and the ball is about to be released. It is in that moment, in the split second before the ball is released, that the bowler is privileged. His balance, the feel of his feet on the ground, his rhythm, his aim, the arch of his back, the movement of his shoulders and the snug sit of the ball in his fingers will tell him in advance about the quality of the ball he is about to deliver. Already Michael is living for that moment when he feels the ripple of the perfect delivery passing through him and he tastes that moment just before it happens. When it is his and his alone, before sharing it with the crowd. In the next frame the ball is released and the remaining two photographs show the smooth, even pacing of Lindwall's follow-through.

Michael has studied these photographs again and again, he has read the great Lindwall's book on the art of the fast bowler. Throughout the summer the ball will hit the back fence above the stumps, and the crack of the impact will reverberate around the neighbourhood like a rifle shot, telling everybody that young Michael is at it again. He has underlined in pencil the most important points in Lindwall's book. At the top of the run, facing the back fence with an old cork ball in his hand, the boy's impulse is always to run in as fast as he can and bowl the ball with all the speed he can gather. But the book tells him to begin slowly, and so, against all instincts, he takes off slowly and doesn't overstretch at the delivery stride because the great Lindwall doesn't.

On these afternoons, while he is slowly increasing his speed, he is vaguely aware of the sounds around him; the children in the yard of the adjacent house, a dog somewhere complaining each time the ball hits the fence, and his next-door neighbour, Mr Barlow, hacking his lungs up into a bucket on his back porch. But these sounds are unimportant. He hears them but they don't concern him because they don't matter.

There is only one sound that matters. The sound of speed. The old cork ball barely leaves his hand when he hears the snap of the impact, sees the ball ricochet off the edge of a fence paling, fly onto the side fence and bounce onto the lawn in front of him. He is aware that the neighbourhood will be listening. He is always aware of the raised eyebrows all around him and the muttered comments that the kid will destroy the fence before he's finished.

During these hours Michael lives in a world of rhythm and action. He aims in turn for each of the painted stumps; the leg, the middle and the off. And he is not content until he hits each of the nominated stumps like the great Lindwall, who impresses the crowds at exhibitions by calling the stump that he hits before bowling the ball.

Occasionally the yelling next door disturbs his concentration. Mr Barlow will have finished coughing his lungs up and his wife will yell at him. She is famous for it. And it is always the same. The house is wrong. The street is ghastly. The suburb is stuck out on the edge of the world. She is ashamed of the address. Ashamed of him. And won't somebody tell that kid next door to stop. She will be yelling all of this while the ball hits the back fence again and again. Then she will cry like she always does, and everything will go quiet once more.

Throughout these repeated episodes of yelling and crying and coughing Michael's eyes are focused on the three stumps painted onto the fence. There are times when he feels almost nothing, neither the weight of his being nor the strain on his legs and back. Times when he is completely oblivious of the instructions flowing from his mind to his body, when he is almost a spectator to his own bowling. And the picture that he sees, from the curve of the back, to the grace of the bowling arm describing its delivery arc and the velvet follow-through, is an exact replica of the great Lindwall in frozen action. And what he sees is made all the more powerful by the certain knowledge that, at the end of such a perfect delivery, there will be damage.

At times like these he is sure he has the gift of speed. And if he does he must nurture it, for in his bones he knows that true speed is a gift. Not something to be squandered and lost. Knows that when a gift is given it must be received with care. And knows that, if he nurtures it properly, it will be speed that will one day carry him along his street, out of the suburb and into the world of the great

Lindwall. This is the importance of being fast, for the kind of speed that turns heads can do all that.

But for the time being he will practise every afternoon in his yard until the fence is shattered and another three white stumps will need to be painted on the remaining palings next to the damaged section. He will follow the instructions of the great Lindwall until action becomes second nature, and the instruments of bowling – his legs, arms, eyes, heart and head – are all one.

When this happens, he will bowl the perfect ball and it will become known as the ball that Michael bowled. The red train will stay just that moment longer in the platform before departing, the mill kittens will cease to gambol, the milk bar owner will look up, suddenly distracted from his lime spider and the dream will meet reality. And even those who don't care much for the game will pause on the footpaths and streets of the suburb in general acknowledgement that this is an event.

6.

The Bruchners

The cigarette butts are piled high in the ashtray beside Mrs Bruchner. She has no sooner finished one than she has started another, the smoke still rising from the last imperfectly stubbed butt.

She is a tall woman, big boned, but plain in the face, with unfortunate breasts that fell flat to her stomach from an early age, and consequently has no figure to speak of, although she is only twenty-nine. Her hands tremble when she raises the cigarette to her mouth to light it. Her hands always tremble, especially when she raises her lighter, which she often does. Even when she smooths her brittle hair, her fingers will sometimes become ensnared in her curls and they will stay there briefly, trembling, until she frees her hand and places it back in her dress pocket where she keeps her lighter.

From her lounge-room window she can see the procession of families passing along the street to the Englishman's house. She is wearing her best summer dress, which hangs loosely over her shoulders and falls undisturbed from her neck to her knees, no swells or curves to invest it with shape. She has long ceased to care about fashion, especially summer fashion. At least in winter she can wrap herself in cardigans and jumpers and feel as if her body has shape. She suffers the summer.

Lipstick stains the filtered tips of the cigarettes and the smoke mingles with her perfume. In her mind she can still hear the dog howling. Her husband, a short, stocky man with a head full of tumbling black curls that he brushes back, with a part down the middle, in the style of a matinee idol from the previous decade, is still in the bathroom. He is broad across the shoulders and chest, with thin, spindly legs. This tapering effect, from shoulders and chest to feet, augments the sense of physical power that he brings to a room, despite his shortness of stature. He is humming to himself now, but all she can hear is the dog.

Every time he feeds the dog, a large Alsatian, he will make it crouch on the grass at the back of the house as he lays a large piece of fresh meat before it. The meat will be no more than a foot away from the dog's nostrils, but the dog will not be allowed to devour it until the instruction is given. And, more than often, Bruchner will keep the dog waiting, especially for the amusement of visitors. Its hind legs will shift about in anticipation and its front paws will claw at the grass while its eyes will look up to Bruchner, listening for the word 'Now'. But he will always keep the dog waiting, pointing to the shifting hind and front legs, and boasting that the dog would never move without his instruction.

Until today. Bruchner, a plasterer, was showing off the ritual to a fellow worker earlier that afternoon. As always, he lay the meat before the crouching animal then stood back, chatting to his visitor as the dog eyed the fresh meat. He won't move, was Bruchner's boast, until I say. And we could stand here all afternoon, Bruchner boasted again, and the dog still won't move. To prove the point they stood before the crouching beast longer than usual, until the dog's front paws began to claw up the grass in front of it to reveal the dirt beneath. And yet still they chatted casually of that Saturday morning's work, pretending to ignore the dog. Then they weren't pretending to ignore the dog any longer, but became intensely involved in a discussion of considerable technical detail. And while they were lost in the details, while they were animated and engrossed in the technicalities of their current contract, the dog suddenly leapt forward and began devouring the meat.

At first Bruchner looked down at the dog in silence, but then he heard the laughter of his workmate as he pointed to the hungry animal, then to his wristwatch, indicating that he'd stayed long enough and that it was time to leave. And it was then that Bruchner first hit the dog with his bare fist. Once, then twice, he hit the dog on the side of the head, then the side of the jaw, for it was now his belief that if the dog could at least be forced to drop the meat from its mouth, then something of his boast might yet be salvaged. And so he belted the dog again until it did, indeed, drop the large lump of meat back onto the lawn. But when Bruchner looked up his fellow worker was already waving goodbye and the dog's subservience went unnoticed.

It was then, with his workmate now strolling along the driveway and out into the street, that Bruchner took a stick that he kept in his shed and set about teaching the dog a lesson.

These are the howls that Mrs Bruchner can still hear as she sits in the lounge room with the piled ashtray beside her, lighting one cigarette after another with her shaking hands.

The beating went on, the dog crouched again whimpering before the semi-chewed meat, taking one blow after another. And even when Joy Bruchner opened the kitchen door and begged him to stop, Bruchner had merely looked up for a moment and replied that the dog must learn, before returning to the beast.

When the beating finally stopped, the dog slouched to a corner at the back of the yard and licked its hind legs and front paws without sound.

That silence, Mrs Bruchner now notes, as she lights another cigarette and listens to Bruchner walk from the bathroom to the bedroom where he will put on the new summer shirt she ironed that afternoon, that silence is almost as disturbing as the howls themselves, just as the stillness that came over the yard afterwards was a menacing stillness.

As he is buttoning up his shirt Bruchner is piecing together the fragments of the afternoon, still puzzled by the dog's actions. For some reason he is going over the conversation he had with his workmate. He had been making an important point. In the past, he said, contracts were often hard to fulfil because materials were hard to come by.

'Now,' he had said, with emphasis and with his finger raised, 'it is no longer the case.'

Bruchner suddenly realises why the dog pounced on the fresh meat. So simple. The dog had waited for the instruction after all, and all he has to do is point that out to his workmate. He will do so on Monday morning. In the meantime the dog will have forgotten all about the beating. And when he steps outside to feed the animal it will bound towards him and crouch low, its hind legs shifting about in anticipation, its front paws clawing at the grass, waiting for the game to begin all over again.

The Bruchner house was constructed in anticipation of children, but no children came. The lounge room is wide, with curved corners, and the floorboards, of the best Tasmanian hardwood, are polished and shiny like glass. The plastered walls are perfectly finished. In the evenings their footsteps echo throughout the house. As she pushes a half-smoked cigarette into the ashtray she can hear Bruchner's approaching footsteps in the hallway, and she realises how much she loathes that sound.

Outside, through the curtains, she sees Vic, Rita and Michael pausing by the paddock opposite. If she weren't so worn out she could have sobbed. Just one, she is noting, just one makes all the difference. Just one more makes a couple a family, and she dwells upon that simple fact as she reaches into her dress pocket for the lighter and Bruchner enters the room.

7

Speed

All through the winter and the spring the paddocks are green and lush with tall grass, thistles, prickles, wild shrubs, wild flowers and red berries. When the paddocks are moist and abundant, Rita can imagine them being part of wide, open country, as they were before the suburb arrived. Skinner's farm, just beyond the next street, is only a hint of what it once was, before the only remaining family member, the ageing snowy-haired son, unmarried and childless, sold most of the land to developers, retaining only the bluestone farmhouse, a few acres and a handful of cattle to keep him interested in life.

He's got a farmer's face, the son. Red and ruddy from being out all day, and his hair is white and springy. He wears old clothes – canvas trousers, collarless shirts, clothes that nobody wears any more, clothes that nobody has worn for years – as he ambles about the street with that slightly pigeon-toed walk, leaning to one side, saying hello to anybody who passes and mumbling to himself as if he's wondering where on earth he is, and what all these people are doing wandering around where his farm used to be. Simple, the suburb says. Too old, too much sun. Harmless enough, but quietly off his head. But Rita knows he's not. He's just outlived his time. Anybody who outlives their time looks funny to everybody else.

Old stock, Vic calls him. A dying breed. Vic talks to him, and Rita's now slowly turning round to Vic. She wants to ask him what they find to talk about. But he's looking away and for a moment she's worried something is wrong again. She is tempted to ask if he's all right, then she sees that his face is calm. He's all right. He's just looking out towards the flour mills and railway station, lost in his thoughts, working towards an observation that he will soon share with her the way he often does. He's not having a turn. She decides to let him be. There's no need to bother him. Not tonight.

It starts way out there, Vic thinks, beyond the mills, beyond the houses. Out where there's nothing but paddocks of Scotch thistle, where the road itself begins. The main road, the one that splits the suburb, and runs in a straight line for over a mile. There's a curve just after the shops, but it's nothing. You can do a lot with a road like that. And it's made too. Paved. The only made road in the suburb.

I never notice where the sound begins when I'm lying in bed at night. A faint glow at the edges of the window from the streetlight on the corner, the bedroom black, no branches swaying in the wind. Nothing. The kind of silence that hums. Suddenly there's a low groan out on the road. Coming from out there, beyond the railway line, and the houses. This low, rumbling groan, tearing along the road.

The engine's got a big note that spills out over the suburb, growing in volume with every second, and I can tell exactly where the car is. I can hear him passing the mills, passing the shops, hear him slow down ever so slightly for the curve at the top of the street, then hear him emerge from the bend and simultaneously put his foot to the floor as he settles into that mile of uninterrupted, straight, flat road.The main road is the next up, parallel to this, and as he passes I know he's moving. I know a thing or two about speed.

There's a brief tremor of sound at the bedroom window, a flutter among the venetians as he passes.

Then he fades into the night as the drive takes him along the entire northern boundary of the golf course.

It's one or two o'clock in the morning. I don't know who he is. Then again I may have met him. But I doubt it. He takes care of that car. It's tuned like a musical instrument. You can tell he's taken it apart and put it back together, again and again. He must have to make a sound like that. He knows every part of it. And when he drives it he can visualise all the moving parts.

I know that much. And I know what takes him out there at this time in the morning. The road is completely his. He can push his car to the very limits. He can either accelerate into life, or accelerate into death, and there's nothing to stop him.

The groan dies at the end of the golf course fence, then suddenly starts again. Back along the length of that thin, black strip of road, past the golf course, past the house, sending another brief shiver through the venetians, and onto the curve at the top of the road where the car slows ever so slightly, begrudgingly, then past the shops and the flour mills, and back out to wherever it was it came from in the first place, till the groan of the engine merges with the hum of the silence that's settled on the bedroom again.

* * *

Two, three times a week Vic hears that sound. He's come to expect it. Come to listen for it. When he wakes at night the silence is everywhere. Until that car comes along and the sound starts again.

Yes, he's all right. She'll leave him alone. Wherever his memories or thoughts have taken him, he wants to go there by himself for the moment. So Rita lets him be. Besides, she's counting the years. He's walking slowly beside her, looking beyond the street out towards the mills, his eyes partially closed like people do when they're listening for something. But what could he be listening for out there? The train's passed. She can't hear anything now. She could ask him, but she's busy counting the years they've been together. Even though she knows, she adds them all up again. Fourteen. Then she counts backwards, all the way back to the first year, the first night. The one that led on to all the others. All fourteen of them.

She'd seen violence before. But not up close. She'd heard stories of violence. Her mama often went into people's houses and looked after those who were too old or too drunk to look after themselves. She'd go with her at nights because she was too young to be left at home alone. When her mama was finished her rounds they'd walk back up Greville Street to the police station where she would report to the police on the drunks and the fights and the alcohol. Sometimes Rita heard about the violence her mama might have seen through the day, but not often. Everybody knew her mama. Whenever they passed the pubs, the drunks outside on the footpaths would stop swearing and fighting, and raise their hats as they passed. So Rita never really saw violence up close until the first time she met Vic.

We were dancing that first time, Vic and me. We'd never met before. We've never danced together before. I can still hear the song, smell the perfume, the aftershave and the soap in that big, stuffy dance hall. Neither of us were talking, then he told me his name, introducing himself, and I liked the sound of it. It sounded right. Just the kind of name I'd been waiting to hear. I was nineteen and felt like I'd been around forever waiting for something to happen. And while I was thinking about the sound of his name I was watching him talk. I wasn't really listening, you can't when you're trying to take everything in at once. But I knew he was trying to be funny and I'd laugh every now and then.

What I noticed was this, he could dance. I mean really dance. And he wasn't afraid to hold me. I could feel his hips and his arms. There was energy there. He was talking away but he was throwing himself into the dancing. He had life, Vic. And all this with his good looks. No wonder I wasn't listening to him. Besides, when he told me his name and it sounded right, I said to myself, this is it. And while I was listening to that voice inside my head, saying this is it, there was another voice telling me I'd never said that before. I'd always been one to um and ah in the past. But not that night. That night it was, well, it was like the movies.

Mama always told me I had a head full of movies. Too many. If I wasn't at one, sitting and dreaming in the dark, I had my head in a movie magazine. I knew all about their lives, all of them. The stars. And mama was always dragging me out of the shops where all the shop owners knew me, saying the movies weren't life. That if the movies were like life nobody would go. Did I understand? And I'd nod. I'd nod as she would lead me off to some dark, old house, where she washed and cleaned all the grey old women who were too old and tired to wash themselves. And I'd sit and help in those old rooms that smelt the way old peoples' houses do, with their drawn curtains blocking the world out, the air heavy and dark, and the bedrooms always stinking with the stale smell of old woman's urine coming up from the potties they kept under their beds. And no matter how much they covered their potties in fine lace doyleys, with flowery borders and glass jewels to weigh them down, the rooms always smelt of urine because they were all too old, too tired and too past it to empty them. So it was left to mama, even though she wasn't much younger than the people she looked after.

So when she told me that the movies weren't life I knew exactly what she was talking about and why she was saying it. I'd nod when she asked me if I understood, but deep down I figured the movies could be life. If you waited. If you believed. So when mama and everybody else said they weren't, I just nodded to keep them all happy while I went on believing.

And I was right. It was happening. There we were dancing like we'd been doing it forever. I'd danced myself right into a movie. The right name, the right face, the right song, whatever it was. Everything was as it should be. And then someone pinched my bottom. I jumped. I knew it wasn't Vic. Impossible. We'd known each other for ten minutes and I knew straight away it wasn't him. So when I jumped I said, someone's just pinched me on the bottom. He said who? I looked around and there was this bloke I'd never met before, dancing with a woman I'd never seen before, smiling and waving at me as they drifted away across the dance floor. While the song was still playing Vic stopped dancing, and walked up to the other couple. And this was when I saw violence up close for the first time.

Afterwards somebody said it was nothing, but it didn't look like nothing to me. At first there was just the three of them, then four, then seven, then I lost count. I stood on the edge of it watching. Me, the one who got her bottom pinched. Not that I could see much because everybody else just kept on dancing. They cleared a space and let the fight work itself out. And it did. Soon Vic came back with his shirt torn, hanging loose out of his trousers. And he was rubbing his hand, telling me it didn't hurt and trying to grin. I was too stunned to do anything but follow him onto the lawn at the front of the dance hall.

Outside the palms were swaying in the wind. Before the fight happened I could have imagined an orchestra under the palms, but now all I could hear was the cold sound of the waves in the bay splashing onto the beach behind the bluestone walls at the bottom of the street. I looked at my watch and it was quarter past nine. By my calculations we started dancing at quarter to. Maybe less. We'd known each other for a little over twenty-five minutes. And when I thought about it like that I told myself I shouldn't feel any compulsion to stay. I asked him if he wanted me to stay, and he said yes. But he didn't want to go back inside, and I said good, I've had enough of dancing.

It was cold as we walked down to the beach. I had a sly smile on my face just for mama. He looked good on the beach in his suit. His coat lapel torn, and his tie still flung over his shoulder. He told me what he did. That's why they called him Vic, not Victor, he said. Vic for Victorian Railways. VR for short. It was a joke. He was standing there talking away, still rubbing his hand, and I was hoping I looked good.

Later, when we walked back up to the dance hall he said can I take you home and I said yes. Yes, you can take me home. Soon, I was sitting up between the handlebars of his bicycle with my legs either side of the front wheel and my dress pulled up so it didn't blow everywhere. He pushed us all the way to South Yarra. All the way up the hill at the end of Tivoli Street. With that salty wind in my face and the tramlines shining before me under the streetlights, I felt like I'd just started to live.

Rita shrugs her shoulders and gives up on the years. It doesn't matter in the end. The years led here. They were always leading here. A new suburb out on the edges of the city. A dirt road, a dirt footpath. The sun low on the swaying grass in the open paddocks. She eyes Vic beside her. His cigarette's gone out and he re-lights one of his cork-tipped cigarettes that he keeps for special occasions. She's watching his hands as he cups the flame. What happens to it all? What happens to all that life? All that time? Where does it all go? One moment you feel like you've got all the years in the world to live, and the next you feel like you've lived them. One moment you can't wait for everything to start, the next you're counting back through the years like it's the only thing left to do.

8.

A Slight Accident

Standing at the corner of the paddock with his back to the Bruchners', Vic stirs as if suddenly waking from a daydream. He motions to the other two who have now fallen behind again and moves forward down the road, aware that his mind has been elsewhere for the last few minutes or seconds, but he is suddenly not sure where or for how long. At these moments the world around him is a puzzle, a surprise. Like it is when you wake from an afternoon doze in a strange place. Familiar faces become a curiosity. Nothing is quite right or real. The street, the houses, his mind. There is *grand mal* and there is *petit mal*. A *petit mal* can last only a matter of seconds, and perhaps that was all the time he drifted off for, but seconds can be eons when the mind goes elsewhere.

* * *

It happens easily enough. It was so cold my fingers were stuck to the handlebars. My bag, slung over my back, kept bumping against my kidneys. The rain had stopped, that bloody awful misty rain that's not even rain, just cloud. I don't mind the rain, real rain, at least it's got a sound. You can hear it, but not that misty stuff, not that morning. I was hunched forward on my bike to keep warm. The light wasn't good and I didn't like the sound of that chain. It was creaking like it was going to snap any minute, like it did the week before. And the last thing I needed going down the hill was for that bloody chain to go on me again. So I was looking at it, watching it, daring it to break. And then it happened.

There was no sound. At least I don't remember one. And I don't remember leaving the bicycle or leaving the road. But suddenly I had a free view of the sky. It was almost relaxing. Part of me said make the most of it, you don't get a view like this too often. And I swear I could see the entire length of the street. The lights hazy in the mist, 'cause that bloody rain had started again. The roofs of the houses, like rows of pyramids in the drizzle. And at that moment I could also see the lights go on in somebody's kitchen and I knew beyond doubt there

was a cup of tea on the way. I could see the new
scout hall, the road junction, the moving headlights
of a few cars out there on the rim of the old river
valley as it winds down to the trestle bridge that I've
crossed time and again with a full load of coal or
ballast behind me and, at the same time, I could see
the point where the houses stop and the darkness of
the paddocks begins. It was all spread out below me
as I slowly turned round in the air. And it was
almost good, almost good to know that everything
was going on without me for the time being. I could
even see my bike, back there on the road, and I
knew I was about to join it again soon. Then I
thought I could see my body back there on the road
too, curled up with the bike and it struck me for the
first time that I might even be bloody well dead.
Well, be buggered with that. I'm not. Not yet. And
suddenly I was in a hurry to get back to my bike,
and that grey shiny road, and a car, half out of its
drive and half in.

The road rose to meet me and the thud as I hit the
ground was enough to wake the neighbourhood. I
could feel my brain move. It just bounced from one
side of my skull to the other and back again. Slapped
up against my forehead like mince into a sheet of
butcher's paper. A car door slammed and someone
was standing over me asking me how I felt. I didn't
say anything, I was just staring at him. I didn't know

how I felt and I rolled my head to one side and noticed my bike and the contents of my bag sprawled all over the road. Funny, I didn't remember my bag leaving me. Yet there it was, and there was my tin billy with the stew inside. The lid was still on so I hadn't lost my lunch. But the sugar jar was broken and my tea was all over the road. My bike was a bit jiggered too. The front wheel was twisted and buckled. The spokes were crooked. The back wheel was still spinning. At least my brain had stopped moving and I wasn't feeling too bad. I could even collect my thoughts, and the first thing that occurred to me was that if I didn't stop lying around I was going to be late for work. But when I tried to get up this bloke who was suddenly kneeling over me now said don't move. Then he ran inside and came out again.

Soon my bike was being dragged off the road and my billy was back in my bag and my bag was back on the footpath. By then I was sitting on the fence looking at what was left of my bike. But I didn't remember getting there, like I didn't remember this other bloke turning up. A doctor, I guess, because he kept asking about my bones and my head, and I told him about my brain bouncing around. Apart from that I told him I felt good. Then I asked the time and mentioned that I was due at work, but this doctor told me I wasn't going anywhere. Then they bundled me into a car with my bag on my lap and the next thing I knew I was sitting up in bloody hospital.

I hadn't had a day off in years and I couldn't help feeling I should be at work. They kept me there all morning, watching me and doing all sorts of tests, then they put me in a taxi home. Everybody was waiting for me when I got there. They looked worried and I told them to relax, that I was all right. The next day I was back on the engines like nothing had happened.

Two years later I woke up one morning and my wife, my son, and the local doctor were all standing round my bed looking at me like I'd just come back from the dead and I knew something was wrong. I'd been dribbling in my sleep and I was sweating all over and my jaw was aching like I'd been clenching my teeth all night. The doctor was asking me if I'd had a fall or knocked my head in the last few years. So I told him. He asked me what day it was, who the prime minister was and I couldn't tell him. Then he asked me my name. Vic. My name's Vic, I said. And I was going to shoot him the usual line but I knew he wouldn't laugh so I left it at that.

That's when he explained what happened. I had no memory of whatever it was, but I knew something happened. He called it a *grand mal*. I said what's that? He explained it to me like it happens every day of the week, and it probably does for him, but not for me. Then he left a prescription and told me to cut back on the grog or the tablets were useless.

When everyone was outside I was still sitting up in bed staring out the window. The first thing I decided on was telling nobody at work. If they found out they'd stop me driving. And I'm not bloody well finished driving yet.

Vic is now walking ahead of the other two, about to leave the open paddock behind. He is drawing quickly on one of the cork-tipped cigarettes he keeps for social outings, so that he doesn't have to roll his own at formal occasions, like he would at work or at the pub.

From the moment he first sat in the drivers' classes at the VR school, from the first time he sat down with *Bagley's Guide* and committed it to memory, page by page, asking himself the questions and chanting the answers in those routine late-night catechisms that preceded his driver's examination, from that moment on words like 'responsibility', 'mastery', 'devotion', 'judgement' and 'principle' had been impressed upon him like key terms of a faith, not a profession. But as much as he knows he shouldn't be driving, he also knows that his dream is now so near he can almost see his name on the Big

Wheel roster. Probably only months, possibly weeks away. To stop now, at this crucial moment, would be a betrayal of a lifetime's driving. He wasn't bloody well finished with engines. Not yet. Even though all his better judgement tells him he should get out now, he can't.

As he strolls along the footpath he hears Rita's voice calling out after him, asking him if he's all right. She sounds concerned and he turns, stops and tells her he's all right. Straight away she relaxes and he smiles. He can't blame her asking, if she feels she has to. But behind the smile he's a bit shitty about the whole business. The family is always watching now, always keeping an eye on him, asking him if he's all right. And he's not shitty with them, not really. He knows they're only worried for him, looking out for him. But it depresses him all the same, like he's not quite the full quid any more. Then he stops, looks up the road as he waits for Rita and Michael, thinks of the party waiting for them, and the mood passes.

9.

The Big Wheel

... under no circumstances should a driver be placed in charge of passenger trains until he has had experience enough to teach him what is the best to do when extraordinary and unexpected conditions prevail.
Human life is too precious ...

Bagley's Australian Locomotive Engine Drivers'
Guide

Paddy Ryan does not look like a big man. Not at first. It's only when he's coming at you, then he does. He is fifty-seven, still with a full head of hair, and has hands that can dwarf a beer glass, when there's a beer to be had, which is often, because Paddy is fond of a beer.

He is walking slowly along the number one platform of Spencer Street Station. It is early evening and Paddy is gazing up at the sky. Paddy doesn't normally concern himself with such things as the sky, but tonight he does. Everybody does; the guard, the young fireman walking behind him, the porter, the ticket collector at the gate and the first of the passengers beginning to pass through the platform gate.

Paddy is a Big Wheel driver. In an hour he will take the main passenger train between Melbourne and Sydney to the New South Wales border. There are one hundred crews on the Big Wheel throughout the State. They take the passenger trains between Melbourne, Sydney and Adelaide. They drive them to the border where the interstate crews take over. They rest overnight in railway huts, and they bring the trains back the next day or the next night, depending on the train. It is every driver's dream to be rostered on the Big Wheel, because the Big Wheel drivers are the best, the elite. They are the artists of the rail system. The steam engines that once hauled the old passenger trains had giant, six-foot driving wheels. The name has been around for a hundred years. If you drive a passenger, you're the best, you're a big wheel. Anybody can haul coal. It is Vic's hope that one day he will join the sacred circle of the Big Wheel. Like Paddy. Paddy is the best of them all and Vic was lucky enough to have been his fireman. There is no better driver to learn the trade from. When the Queen was here, it was Paddy who drove her train. There are no bumps on Paddy's journeys, no unnecessary swaying from side to side, no sudden jolts. You can eat your meal in the buffet car when Paddy is driving and your plate will stay in front of you, your cup of tea will stay at rest where you last put it. The dips in the track, the need to ease off the throttle, the increase in speed or the need to apply the brakes will all go unnoticed by the passengers on Paddy's trains. Paddy, Queen's driver, has the artist's touch. A driver is born with the feel that Paddy has for engines, wheel and track, and when he is driving at his best, when he is flying, when driver and machine are one, Paddy is utterly still and silent, seven hundred tons of iron and steel responding to the tips of his fingers.

Vic was Paddy's fireman. Seven years they were together. Seven years of watching, listening and taking notes. Seven years of learning the trade from the best there is. How to listen to the engine, how to read the rails. But more than all of this, more than the trade, Vic learnt that to be a great driver you have to bring something of yourself to the task. You have to stamp your work with your individual signature, so that anybody with eyes and ears for the trade will recognise it. For when something is given to engine driving that wasn't there before that driver came along, driving becomes an art.

Paddy is an artist. His great contribution to the trade is his ability to eliminate the bumps that come from the dips in the rails, from sleeper and sleeper, the ballast between the rails will slip and whole sections of rail will dip. But Paddy eliminates these dips and nobody knows how he does it. Not even Paddy. It is the part of Paddy's driving that can't be explained, and it is also that part of Paddy's driving that makes him an artist.

But, at the moment, Paddy is not thinking about any of this. He is watching the sky as he walks to his engine. He is not a man given to much contemplation of the sky, but he is currently asking himself if he has ever seen a sky quite like this. It is the kind of sky that causes people to break their stride, and stop whatever they're doing, if only for a moment. And Paddy stops, taking in the length of the train as he does.

His train is freshly cleaned, and the royal blue of the carriages with their gold lines above and below the window and the distinctive gold lettering, gleam under the platform lights. Set in the enclosed rounded end of the parlour-observation car is the illuminated sign that proclaims the name of the train, *Spirit of Progress*.

From the moment it began service in the thirties it has been the elite passenger train of the country, indeed, famous throughout all those parts of the world where people care about trains. But, for all this, it is simply known in the trade, by the drivers, the firemen, the guards and the passengers, as the *Spirit*.

There are eleven air-conditioned carriages, five first class, three second class, a dining car, the parlour-observation car that bears its name and a luggage van. Eleven carriages, four hundred passengers, two guards, five conductors, the fireman and Paddy. And the engine. But not steam. In the old days the *Spirit* was drawn by streamlined steam engines that were the toast of the Victorian Railways. Paddy is driving one of the new S class diesels. In recognition of the high regard in which this train is held, the new diesels all bear the same names as the original steam engines that have only recently been retired from service and sold for scrap. The brass lettering on the side of Paddy's diesel reads *Sir Thomas Mitchell*.

10.

Albert Younger

There are voices behind them. Rita, Michael, and finally Vic, all glance backwards to the golf course end of the street as they continue their walk down to the Englishman's house. They can't see their own house from here, but they can see the pale gums that run along the edge of the golf course. The wire fence that follows the western boundary of the course is rotted and falling down, a barrier to no one. Michael and his friends from the street are always in that vast, open park even though they know they're trespassing. The wooden gate through which they pass, onto the sandy pathway that leads out to the first tee and the cream and green weatherboard clubhouse on the left, has long since fallen down and its rotted frame now lies on the pine-needle bed beside the fence. Built just before the first war, the whole course is in a slow state of collapse.

Vic, Rita and Michael momentarily fix their eyes on that luminous row of ghost gums, as if half-expecting them to suddenly uproot themselves and join the slow moving procession of families strolling towards the house at the bottom of the street, when there is a faint, metallic click in the night.

Albert Younger has just closed the front gate behind him, and, with his wife, Mary, is now walking along the thin dirt footpath. He wears a starched white shirt, a black tie, and navy blue suit trousers. He is a small, slight man, while Mary is a dark haired, creamy skinned, dark eyed Irish woman. She is twenty-seven and already has five children.

Their house is constructed from wood, cement sheet and pressed boards. It's crowded and Albert is building a new room. He's been building it for a year in his spare hours after work. Every night he walks home, a kitbag in one hand and something for the house under the other arm. Sometimes it's a plank of wood, sometimes a square of masonite, a roll of lino, a tile, a quarter tin of paint or a bag of nails. Bits and pieces. Somebody else's scraps. Some other family's leftovers, the off-cuts and discards of another home, left lying around the construction sites after the builders have gone.

Every night he carries a piece of his home back with him. And if he meets somebody in the street on his walk from the station, his steps always long and evenly spaced as if he were constantly pacing out the measurements of this room and all the other rooms he would eventually need to build, he lowers his head as he responds to their greetings quietly. When the children of the street say, 'Hello, Mr Younger', eyeing off the salvaged material he is carrying, he nods with his eyes still on his feet as if not wishing to interrupt an important calculation.

Even now, as he walks arm in arm with his wife towards the Englishman's house, Albert Younger is counting his steps.

By winter, bit by bit, piece by nailed piece, the room will be finished. And it won't have cost him a penny. Not even the paint, a dark green, military mixture that will cover all the awkward joints, the jigsaw of shapes and the varying textures of the planks and boards. But no sooner is the room complete than another becomes necessary. Albert Younger is always striding back from the station with a piece of his house under his arm.

When a flyscreen door snaps in the night, Vic turns around and quickly recognises a familiar voice carrying across to him from the other side of the street. The door snaps again and a family, the

Millers, assembles on the porch of the house directly in front of them. Everybody waves to each other and the young family of four, in bright, starched clothes, walks in unison to the front gate and steps onto the footpath. The two families then walk parallel to each other on different sides of the street, exchanging greetings, glances and nods.

The husband's name is Doug. He's a machinist at a nearby factory, in another suburb. He's the happiest married man in the street, but he will die the next week in a car accident. He smiles and waves again before turning to his wife. Under the last of that peach sky they're safe. Nothing can touch them. They stop as the young girl kneels and adjusts her sandal. There are no fates to be met because no one's moving. But as soon as the girl finishes adjusting her sandal, they're off again, moving forward to that moment, a few hours later next Saturday, when a carload of drunks will drive through a red light.

He's twenty-eight, she's twenty-four. He's just bought her a small, stone pendant, especially for this night. But as much as she loves that pendant, she'll never wear it again. Within weeks the house will be sold and a new family will arrive.

As they walk Rita glances at the young wife, Nell. Being almost ten years older she thinks of her as a young wife, a young mother, and she sees the contentment in her face, her gestures. A serene confidence that all the days and all the nights will go on just as they are now, and that the course of their lives will simply unroll like new lino, tapering to a distant point too far away to bear thinking about.

You may think your life goes on forever Mrs Miller, Rita is thinking as she watches them. But I'm thirty-three and you make me feel old. I'm thirty-three and I can see that there will be an end to it all. And, Mrs Miller, nothing frightens me more. Being dead. Cooped up in a box. All alone. Everybody going on as usual, without you. But what else can they do except go on as usual? Rita glances at Vic who is reading the hands of his railway fob watch. I'm thirty-three and she makes me feel old. Why is that? Vic closes the face of the watch, slips it into his pocket and stares ahead as if calculating the minutes that must be made up if they are to ease into the platform of the Englishman's house on time.

The Millers are still standing on the other side of the street. Looking back up towards the golf course again, Rita nods to the approaching figures of Albert Younger and his wife. The curved brick corners of the Bruchners' house are indistinct. The thin, pale figure of Joy Bruchner, if she's not already at the party, will be chain-smoking inside. Sometimes, when Rita passes her house, Mrs Bruchner is sitting outside on the porch steps staring down at her feet, or gazing at the dried lawnseeds that never took root. But when Michael says hello, she immediately looks up, often running her fingers through her hair to smooth it down, to smarten herself up a bit before she returns the greeting. At these moments Rita sees the brittlest of smiles, the saddest trace of light in Mrs Bruchner's eyes, as if she is counting herself lucky enough to have brushed with some blessed normality.

II.

Patsy Bedser

On a dull Saturday afternoon the previous autumn, Patsy Bedser drove into the countryside north of the suburb, into the river valley and through the small farming towns and hamlets it contains.

The street along which she drove had no trees, like most of the streets in the suburb, for they were cleared away to make room for the houses. There were no leaves on the ground and no sign that it was autumn apart from the misty rain and the still air. She drove her pale green Morris Minor from the street, where she had lived for the last five years since leaving England with her father, and steered it towards the hills, and the old township road that eventually led into the countryside.

As she watched the street recede in the rear-vision mirror, she realised how much she hated it and how happy she was to be leaving it, if only for the afternoon. The plain and ugly weatherboard houses, some painted, some still left with only a slapped-on undercoat, the bare yards, the pathetic gardens, the dirt road like a cattle track, the vacant lots and the wide open paddocks, caught between farm and suburb. She wished they'd never come. She was a city girl, from Liverpool. Not a big city, but city enough. And this was a frontier settlement. But they were ten pound Poms, the boat ticket only took them one way, and there was nothing else for it but to see the whole thing through.

At the flour mills she crossed the railway lines and turned right into the suburb's other major road. One ran east west, the other north south. Where they intersected they divided the suburb, like a T-square, into three separate regions. The road that ran north south led to the old neighbouring township and the army camp. There were a few houses along that mile-and-a-half drive, but once she passed the old township she entered the open country.

At a curve in the country road she had chosen to travel, she stopped at a deserted bluestone church at the top of a small river valley, just before the road descended to the narrow bridge that forded the stream.

She parked the car and sauntered towards the church, which was set well back from the road. There was a mixture of gums, elms and slender birches all around her and the bright, fallen leaves were sodden under her feet, almost slippery, and she was careful as she walked.

When a black Austin Wolseley pulled into the road siding behind her she looked over her shoulder briefly, then turned back to the sight of the sun in the trees. Even when the car door slammed she stayed staring at the sun.

A young man with long legs and black pointy boots and a loping, cowboy stride was walking towards her. A hi-fi salesman. He sold her a hi-fi a couple of months before, but the thing didn't work. She called him back and they'd no sooner finished discussing the problem with the hi-fi, when they found themselves talking about music. Real music. Eddie Cochran. Gene Vincent. He took the thing away and brought it back a few days later. It worked for a week then stopped again and she called him back again. It happened three times and every time their conversations went a little longer. Eventually she said he must be sabotaging the thing. 'And why would I be doing that?' he said. Patsy shook her head. She was going out with a local plumber. They met every Saturday night and went to the pictures and watched whatever was on. They rarely went out through the week because he was too busy. He was setting up a business and rose early on workdays. Patsy was happy enough with it all, until she met Jimmy, the hi-fi salesman.

It had been mid week. Late afternoon. She remembered the details clearly. Patsy was home early from work at the hospital. She was a nurse. Her dad was still at the docks. There she was standing on the front steps, talking to this Jimmy again. She was flirting and she knew it. He had just asked her why he would do such an unethical thing as sabotage the hi-fi. She didn't reply. And when the young man repeated his question with a bit of a grin on his lips this time, she said it must be because he liked their talk and all, and that every time he took the hi-fi he fixed the old problem but created a new one so he could come back again.

It was a joke, a long shot. But there was an awkward silence afterwards and she wished she'd never opened her big mouth. So when the young salesman eventually nodded and said that was right, she laughed. Then she saw he wasn't laughing. The grin was gone from his lips and he was just looking at her, openly, staring like there was no need for games any more, and she knew he wasn't joking.

That's how it all started. They see each other

every week. But, whatever it is they've got, she knows it's not for keeps. He's a bit like his hi-fis, this Jimmy.

They weren't looking for the old church the first time they drove out to the country together. But they found it. There were weeds and wild flowers growing from the gaps in the bluestone, and it was tucked away under the trees, but they found it all the same. And when she followed his black Wolseley into the siding that first afternoon they came here, a still autumn day of brilliant sunshine, she knew exactly what she was doing. They both did. It didn't take much to snap the lock on the door. A quick look around to make sure nobody was watching and they were inside.

It became their hideaway. During the week, nobody ever went there. A perfect sanctuary. Only a half an hour from the suburbs, but it was another world. It was also another Patsy who went there.

When the young man's long legs finally crossed the siding and reached Patsy, who was still staring at the sun coming through the trees, he simply spun her around by the shoulder, without a word, and they were dancing. He was singing too. He knew all the latest songs because the records came in with the hi-fi's and they played them in the store whenever they got the chance. The young people, that is. The oldies turned up their noses. But that, he said, was only because they weren't far away from turning up their toes. He's got a cheek this one, thought Patsy. And he can sing.

He danced her in through the doorway of the old church, spinning her around in circles and singing something about a teddy bear. When they were inside his voice bounced and echoed all around that empty church, and Patsy, who was all too aware of having been a good girl all her life, was breathless.

Now, she's running from the kitchen to the lounge room and back again, carrying plates and cutlery and paper serviettes. Her father, George, is enjoying a quiet moment in the kitchen before everything begins. The plumber, to whom she is becoming engaged this night, is arranging chairs in the lounge room before putting music on the hi-fi. At the moment they are the only occupants of the house. But the guests are already making their way down the street and within minutes they will be standing in the hallway, lounge and kitchen of the house, and everything will begin.

12.

The Grand Mal

Vic, Rita, Michael and the Millers continue their conversation as they walk parallel to each other along their respective dirt footpaths. Two families, speaking to each other across the street. Michael has nothing to say and is watching his father commenting on the night and the sky, when he stops in mid-sentence, as if he can't remember what to say next. As if the tracks of his thoughts had run out. He even stops in his stride and looks back to Rita and then Michael, passing the sentence over to them to complete, while he remembers what he meant to say.

But Michael's lost in his own memories. Somewhere about him he hears the voice of his mother talking to their neighbours, his father still has a puzzled, lost look on his face, and his mother is constantly glancing at him as she talks. Their voices are quiet and clear like chimes.

But they soon fade into silence, and the street dissolves under Michael's feet. Michael has seen that lost look on his father's face before. He knows it all too well now. The last time, a few months before, he had had to unmuddle his father's mind so that the lost look would go away from his eyes.

Michael had been woken by the alarm clock in his parents' room. It was early in the morning, dark and cold, and outside the rain was falling softly on the roof of the house as it had been all night. He closed his eyes and imagined it falling all over the suburb, on all the roofs and all the houses, on the golf course greens, the fairways, the clubhouse, the school and the dirt streets. Fine, steady, invisible rain, except when caught by the streetlights.

In his parents' room the alarm clock was still ringing and he knew his father hadn't stirred. His mother was away travelling in the country. For the whole week she would be travelling from country town to country town demonstrating washing machines to the audiences in the large country stores. In the front room the alarm was still ringing and he knew he would have to get up and wake his father himself or he would be late for work.

But it was cold and the sound of the rain on the roof outside made him want to stay in bed. He sank down into the warmth of the bed and rubbed his feet together. The alarm was beginning to wind down. Its ringing slowed, then faded altogether. His father had slept through the whole thing and Michael knew he would have to get up then or he would fall back into sleep himself.

Before he could change his mind he threw the blankets back and his bare feet hit the floor. He crossed the room, opened his door and stomped into the hallway which was heavy with the stale smell of last night's beer and cigarettes. He switched the light on and stood, adjusting his eyes to the glare. There were bottles on the kitchen table and a large, filled ashtray. It was always the same when his mother was away.

He slapped on the light in his parents' room and shook his father till he woke. His father's eyes opened slowly and he looked about the room, trying to establish where on earth he was, then turned to Michael, scrutinising his face for a moment and pronounced Michael's name. It was a question, a statement, a greeting, all in one. His father's eyes were now open, but his mind was muddled. Michael could see that. He went to the kitchen, brought back a chair, and sat by his father's side. From previous experience he knew it would take time to unmuddle his father's mind.

'You slept through the alarm.'

'Did I?'

His father spoke with disbelief, as if he had never slept through an alarm before.

'It's four-thirty.'

'Is it?'

'Do you know what shift you're on?'

His father sat up and rested his head back against the bed. He was staring blankly across the room, running his forefinger down along the bridge of his nose, but the answer wouldn't come. Eventually, he turned to Michael and shook his head. There was fear in his eyes, like the fear of a frightened, confused child, and Michael knew he would have to speak slowly and clearly if he was going to unmuddle his father's mind. He would have to speak to him like a child and he didn't want to because his father was not a child. Michael was the child, he knew that. All his friends wanted to grow up fast so they could be old enough to drive cars, smoke cigarettes and leave home. But Michael wanted to be his age, to act his age, and stay a child as long as he could. But his father was staring back at him with confused eyes and Michael knew he would have to stop being a child for a little while, and speak to his father slowly and clearly, so that his memory could come back and his mind could be good again.

'You're on the morning shift,' Michael said.

'Am I son?'

'You start at six. Do you want me to call Ed?'

Vic looked at Michael blankly.

'Who?'

Michael looked to the window and the faint, silvery streetlight outside, then turned back to his father.

'You don't know who Ed is?'

His father clasped his hands together and looked down to them as if praying, but the memory wouldn't come and he looked up to Michael ashamed that he didn't know the answer.

'Ed is your fireman. He's been your fireman for three years. He's been to dinner here. Ed.'

His father slapped the side of the bed as the memory returned.

'Yes. Ed.'

'Shall I call Ed?'

'No,' his father said in a sudden panic, 'Don't call him.'

'Do you know what time you start?'

'What time do I start, boy?'

'Six. It's a goods train.'

'Where to?'

Michael named the town and his father smiled and nodded at him.

'Yes. That's it. That's right.'

Michael leaned back in his chair. Sometimes the process took longer, sometimes it took less. It all depended. The alertness returned to his father's eyes and Michael knew he would be all right. His mind had been cleared and his eyes were no longer those of a confused child. He thanked Michael for waking him and Michael returned the chair to the circular wooden table in the kitchen and stumbled back into the darkness of his bedroom where he lay listening to the faint, steady rain falling on the roof.

Soon, there was the distant tinkling of a teaspoon in a cup and he knew that, after having cleared away the evidence of the night's drinking, his father would sip black tea in the kitchen with the wireless turned low so as not to disturb Michael.

Later the back door opened, the cat, curled up and sheltering from the rain on the back step complained at being shifted, and Michael heard his father wheeling his bicycle along the gravel driveway. It was too early for the first train and his father would ride his bicycle from their suburb to the North Melbourne yards.

He pictured the hunched figure of his father disappearing along the dirt road in the rain, navigating the potholes and puddles by the sparsely placed streetlights. And he recalled the local doctor speaking very quietly in the kitchen one morning to Michael and his mother. He had spoken slowly so as not to assume anything and an important lesson be understood.

Michael had woken that morning, a year ago, to the sound of his mother's screams. She was calling out his father's name, again and again, and Michael had rushed into his parents' bedroom to see his mother standing by the bed, his father straining for breath and froth coming from his mouth. Later, the doctor had arrived, examined Vic, and that was when he had sat Michael and his mother down in the kitchen and explained to them what had happened.

At one point the doctor had spoken in French. These, he explained, were medical terms, but said in French. There was *grand mal* and there was *petit mal*. Michael's father had just suffered a *grand mal*. It was frightening to watch, but as long as he took his medication and didn't drink he would be all right. The *grand mal* was more frightening than the *petit mal* because it lasted much longer and looked worse. A *petit mal* might last only a few seconds, or even minutes, like a sudden memory loss. It quickly passed.

But during that time the mind would be muddled. Thoughts and messages would be sent to the mind but make no sense. The memory would be lost for a short time, and Vic would need help to unscramble his mind and make it right again. During that time, the doctor added, he will be frightened because there will be a part of his mind that knows that the rest of it is muddled.

There was an old wooden spoon in the kitchen drawer for when it was worse. For when his father suffered a big fit, and would not wake until the fit was finished. It could go on for an hour or more. The doctor had told him that during that time, when his father was unconscious, there was the danger that he might swallow his own tongue and choke on it. It hardly ever happened, the doctor reassured Michael and Rita, but it could. For during these fits, the doctor went on, his father's jaw would shut tight like a steel trap. His teeth would be clamped together, they would grind against each other, froth would bubble from his lips and he would moan as if he were in pain. But he wouldn't be. They would have to remember that. It always looked worse than it actually was, and when his father woke he would be tired more than anything, and his jaw would ache.

Because he is already the stronger of the two, Michael's job during these times, and it is nearly always in the early morning, is to take the old wooden spoon that is kept in the kitchen drawer and prise his father's mouth open so that the spoon sits in between his front teeth and keeps his father's tongue in place, so that he won't swallow it and he won't choke. He must be careful that he is not bitten, not that his father will mean to bite him, but sometimes his jaw will suddenly snap shut despite Michael's best efforts. These are the worst times, and it is Michael's job to sit by his father's side throughout the fit. Till his jaw relaxes, his eyes open, and he returns to consciousness.

This morning was easy. Michael lay back in the darkness of his room, alone in the house, thinking about all this. His father had just had a *petit mal*. That was why he didn't know the details of the day. And that's why his eyes were confused and frightened, because he knew that his mind had briefly gone and he could never be sure he would get it all back again; his mind, and the world, the lifetime of memories it contained.

Done with all the talk of the sky and the warmth of the night for the time being, the conversation in the street stops and the two families move forward again in parallel lines towards the Englishman's house. Soon, they will be at the Bedser's party and they can already hear the faint sounds of music issuing from the opened windows of the house and pouring out into the warm suburban air.

Michael is looking forward to the party, to the ice cream and cakes and lemonade. But he is also thinking of those nights when he sits by his father's side waiting for the fits to pass or unmuddling his mind, and wishing it didn't happen.

13.

Diesel and Steam

The deep rich blue of the engine, the long, sweeping yellow line along each side, the yellow crest at the front like that of a magnificent bird about to take flight, and the VR insignia at the centre of it all.

Paddy likes the new diesels, but he keeps it quiet. Many of the drivers still prefer the steam, but Christ only knows why. They say there's no art in the diesels. No heart. It's just a job now and everybody might as well be driving buses, that only steam had that touch of class, of poetry, and that the diesels marked the end of the true art of engine driving.

But Paddy smiles at the drivers who say all this. In the sheds and the yards and standing by the rails at the change of shifts they talk a lot about steam and diesel.

Paddy quietly smiles at their fear of the new diesels and their pronouncements about the end of true driving. There's an art to driving them all, he tells himself, as he stands on the platform beside the diesel with his Gladstone bag at his feet. It's just a different kind of driving.

The diesels are clean and warm from the moment you step inside. No filthy coal, no cinders, no muck all over your face and hands, no rain and wind and sudden gusty drafts. None of that. Just a warm, clean cabin in which to work and a soft seat on which to park yourself.

Paddy takes another look at the sky then picks up his bag and steps up into the cabin. He places his cigarettes in the breast pocket of his overalls. The overalls are no longer really necessary, but Paddy still wears them. Like the faded blue cap he wears when driving, the overalls are his uniform. They are also his link with the past, for although he approves of the new diesels, he is also a sentimentalist. For the same reason he also wears a collar and tie under his overalls. He has done so since he first entered the Big Wheel in 1936. It is a reminder of the days when engineers were as revered by children and admired by the public as airline pilots. Paddy remembers the days when to be an engine driver was that important.

When all the drivers sat at their seats in shirts and ties, and the confidence and assurance they exuded flowed back through the whole train and everybody, even the most apprehensive passengers, were put at ease. A driver should have that effect on a train. So that when passengers and well-wishers gather round the engine to glimpse the driver inside the cabin, they see a professional with the unhurried manner of someone who has complete confidence in his ability.

Paddy sits and nods to his fireman. He is a new fireman and his name does not automatically register with Paddy. Besides, he'll be gone soon, driving himself before he really knows how. Routine takes over. Paddy checks the brake valves, the brake travels and the lighting, while his fireman makes sure the detonators, the tool kit and the headlamp are all there. By now the platform is filling up with travellers and well-wishers, those who have come to wave the passengers goodbye, those who will miss them and those who are glad to see the last of them, all stand peering in through the carriage windows. Paddy eases himself into the soft driver's seat and positions himself for the drive. When he has adjusted the side window, he takes a tea-stained metal mug from his Gladstone bag behind him on the floor and passes it to the fireman.

The fireman takes the mug and a packet of tea. He then opens a hatch and steps down into the nose of the engine. It is only a few steps, but while the fireman is there preparing the tea, he can see nothing of the world outside or of the cabin just above him. Nor can he hear anything. He is completely cut off. When he has finished making the tea he takes two mugs back up into the cabin where the two men sit in silence, sipping the brew. Without the fireman noticing Paddy swallows a small, white pill, then observes once more the miraculous, beery glow of the summer sky hanging over the Spencer Street yards, noting the way it tints the rails and washes over the sheds and signal boxes and turns the clouds to froth.

At six twenty-eight the platform staff are closing all the doors. The train is full. The platform is crowded. Two minutes later the *Spirit* slowly eases out of the platform into those amber yards and on towards North Melbourne Station.

From now until they reach the border the minutes don't matter. There is no wish to be somewhere else, no desire for time to quickly pass into the future or roll back into the past. There is only the job at hand and Paddy is at his happiest. He is doing the job he was born for and over the next few hours he will become lost in its intricacies.

14.

The Arrival of a Bicycle

The music of Bedser's party becomes clearer. It is old music. Old songs. His parents' music. Michael imagines the sleepy eyes of Mr Bedser waiting for his guests. He thinks of the daughter for whom the party is being held. The Patsy Bedser he knows from the milk bars of the suburb and its streets. The familiar Patsy Bedser. Then he thinks of the other Patsy Bedser, the one he discovered on his bicycle late last summer.

When Michael's bicycle arrived a year ago, it arrived in bits. A frame painted in green house paint, rusted handlebars, and wheels from separate bicycles. It didn't matter. Like a jigsaw everything fitted eventually and he spent the afternoon assembling the parts that would become his bicycle, greasing the chain and the sprockets, shining the spokes, tightening the handlebars and adjusting the seat. When it was finished and he'd pumped the air into the tyres, he stood it up against the clothesline in the back yard and contemplated it.

A bicycle meant freedom. He could travel beyond the street, beyond the suburb. He could cycle into the countryside, to the old towns and out to the valleys and streams and rivers where the fish were. Or he could just sit in an open field and eat sandwiches. A bicycle meant all that.

Soon, he knew all the towns, the farms, the yabby dams and the streams. Anywhere that was within a day's ride of the street. The farms through which you couldn't walk because the farmers wouldn't let you; the houses where the dogs ran at you. He eventually came to know it all. Even where the small roads led. But, in the end, it wasn't a fishing spot that he found.

One day the previous autumn Michael was cycling up a long, difficult hill. His fishing rod was strapped to his bicycle and his pack was on his back. It was a school holiday and he was looking forward to fishing in one of the cold, clear streams in the countryside beyond the suburb. There were redfin in those streams and he intended bringing some home with him that evening.

He had been cycling for almost two hours, but because he left early, before the street had stirred, there was still mist and fog in the hollows and valleys he crossed along the way. There was a small valley further inland, near an old church where the water was clear and swift, and it was possible to see the fish. He had seen the place before on a previous trip, noted the river as he crossed the bridge, seen the large schools of redfin in the water, and determined on returning with his fishing tackle.

But it was further out than he recalled, and as he approached every turn in the road he expected to find the old church, his landmark, before him, but he didn't. Perhaps he was on the wrong road. Perhaps he didn't know all the roads and tracks of the area as well as he thought. He was even considering stopping, at the point of calling the whole expedition off, when he turned into yet another curve in the road and the bluestone church was suddenly in front of him.

There were two cars parked in the siding. A pale green Morris Minor and a black Wolseley. He leaned his bicycle against a tree and looked about but couldn't see anybody. Without knowing why, he was wary. He was convinced that two parked cars in a deserted part of the countryside in the middle of the day meant something. When he looked more closely at the cars he realised he knew one. The

Morris. He was sure it was the pale green Morris Minor owned by Patsy Bedser.

He walked slowly forward, crouching as he crossed the wide expanse of the dirt siding. The church door had been left open, and although he knew he shouldn't approach it, he did.

They were almost directly in front of him. Ten feet away. No more. But they didn't see him. It was dark inside the church but he could just make her out, on an old pew that had been left behind and pushed up against the wall. At first, they were like two shadows crawling over each other in the dark. So quiet you wouldn't know they were there. She was facing Michael, who had frozen in the church doorway, but her eyes were on the ceiling and she didn't notice him. And even though her eyes were wide open she didn't appear to see anything at all. The man had his back to Michael. His hands were inside Patsy Bedser's dress and hers were around his neck. It was hard to tell where their legs were. Besides, Michael only got a glimpse before he darted back from the light of the open doorway and flattened himself against the outside wall of the church.

A glimpse was enough. That was it. That was what it looked like. All legs and arms in the dark. And quiet. Like they didn't want to be found out. Like they didn't want anybody to know they were doing it because they weren't supposed to be. The man looked like he could have been quietly strangling her. And he could have been, no more than ten feet away on the other side of the church door. But Michael knew full well that something other than strangulation was taking place in the shadows of the doorway. He'd have loved to look again, properly, to see what it looked like but he heard a low whisper. The voice of Patsy Bedser. The sound of clothes. The sound of the man. Only the wall separated them from Michael. They were whispering to each other in the old church and their whispers echoed like prayers. He could almost distinguish the words they were saying and wondered if they could hear his breathing. Then came the laughter. Loud and musical. The unbuttoned laughter of Patsy Bedser.

Michael barely dared to breathe in its wake. His hands and legs were still. He didn't know then that he was calm because his fear was buried deep down in his shoes where it wouldn't affect him. He moved along the side wall of the church, conscious of the sound of his shoes on the gravel and constantly looking about him as he left. Once he reached the end he saw the flat, open expanse of land, the dirt siding that he had to cross in order to reach his bicycle. There was no sign of anybody, and after waiting, Michael judged his moment, and ran, expecting at any moment to be seen, hear a voice or footsteps following him.

It was the look on Patsy Bedser's face that he took with him as he scrambled back up the path with his pack still on his back. Whenever he saw Patsy Bedser on the street or in the milk bar she smiled. She always said hello and made little jokes to which he could never think of a response. But he wasn't meant to. He's just a kid, he knows that and his shuffling silence is expected. That was the Patsy Bedser he knew. The Patsy Bedser who inhabited milk bars, the only person he knew who made him want to be older, who made him want to grow up fast so that when she made her little jokes he would know exactly what to say and she would see him as being more than just a kid. But the Patsy Bedser he had just observed was someone else.

When he looked again he saw that the church door had been closed. Michael ran towards his bicycle, took it from the tree he had left it resting against not long before, and cycled away as quickly as he could, occasionally looking back over his shoulder, noting the details of the place and fixing them in his memory. And it was only then that he felt the trembling swelling up from his shoes, into his knees and legs, flowing along his spine, into his shoulders and arms and down into his hands and fingertips. He knew if he kept his eyes fixed on the road before him, if he gripped the handlebars firmly with both hands and if he peddled hard, he would ride the trembling out of his body.

* * *

Later that afternoon when he arrived home he told his father about the day but left out the church. His father was pouring stew into a tin billy for the night shift. When his father left for work Michael waved goodbye but he was distracted. His bicycle was up against the front fence and he was flicking the pedals around with his foot, watching them spin.

Now, as he recalls the musical laughter that came from inside the church that afternoon, he knows that its music was not like the music he can faintly hear coming from Bedser's lounge room. Not the music of his parents. No, Patsy Bedser's laughter that day had been loud and exciting, like the loud music he hears in the hi-fi shop.

15.

Pay Day

I leave the city behind me every night after work when I take the northbound train. As we leave the station I watch the river, the bridge and the park, the palms and trees on the other side of the bridge recede. Even now I think I've caught the wrong train. My city is still south of the river.

All my streets, my laneways, my shops, my picture theatres, my magazine stalls with their latest movie gossip and my green, trimmed parks, all my memories, are now on the other side of the city. On warm, summer nights I would walk back from work through the gardens all the way to Prahran and into the wide, spacious house that mama bought, with my face in a movie magazine. That was me.

My sisters all stayed south of the river, the river that slips away from me every night when my train leaves the platform and we curve across the city to Spencer Street, North Melbourne, Newmarket and on. When, at the end of the suburban line, I see the flour mills in front of me towering over the flat paddocks and square houses, I should feel like I'm coming home but I don't. And when I step off the train and see the wide, open paddocks and the timber houses, looking like they could all be swept away by a good storm, I still wonder what I'm doing here.

Rita looks at the Millers on the other side of the street. They should feel like neighbours but they don't. The street should feel like home, but it doesn't. They are all going to the party, and they all have the party in common. But it's not enough. And as she eyes Vic, and Michael, who is suddenly catching up to them after having fallen behind, she wonders if the street will ever feel like home.

Don't marry him they all said. Everybody. My mother, his mother, his aunts. All four of them. They all said don't marry him. Naturally, I married him.

There I was standing out front of that poky little place in South Melbourne. I was standing on the footpath, the rain was pouring down, but I hadn't even bothered to open my umbrella. He was lying in the gutter in front of me. Face down. I knew he drank a bit. But there he was, passed out. It occurred to me that he might drown, that I should shift him, but I couldn't move myself, let alone him. Pound notes were floating along the gutter and his mother was hurrying after them, picking them up before they washed down the drain. And when she'd slipped the sopping wet notes into her dress pocket she turned back to Vic trying to get him onto his feet. She spoke to him slowly, a parent addressing an overgrown child. All her movements were the movements of someone who'd done it all before.

I'd been sitting in that little lounge room, waiting for him all night with his mother and his aunt. Vic and I were getting engaged and I'd come to have tea and talk about it all. But after an hour he still hadn't come. After two his mother looked down at the cakes and tea and asked me over and over again if I wanted another cup. Vic's aunt was just looking on and saying nothing. But she had the look of someone who knew what was happening.

Eventually, she said it was pay day. Pay day? What does that mean I asked her, and his mother said it didn't mean anything. But she added that Vic could be late, so why didn't I go home and everybody could have tea another time. But I wanted to stay. I was worried.

That was when we heard this sound at the door. A sort of clawing, like a dog or an animal of some kind asking to be let in. The next thing I was standing on the footpath in the rain and he was lying in the gutter with his pay floating all around him.

Dressed in black, in a dark hat and long coat, his aunt waved an umbrella at me. Don't marry him, she called out through the rain. Mark my words, she called as she disappeared up the street, you'll rue the day. And then she was gone around the curve at the top of the road and somehow I'd moved and I was helping his mother walk Vic into the house. We dumped him on his bed and she turned to me, very patient and quiet. Thank you, she said. Quietly. You've been most helpful, but you can leave me now. I'll look after him, and she started to unlace his shoes. I still hear her voice. I walked back to the lounge-room table, to the tea, and the uneaten cakes. I heard her voice yesterday in the summer rain outside the station as I stood watching the lolly wrappers being washed along the gutter in front of me, and I hear it now, in this street, under a wide, warm sky. I still hear her voice, soft and sad, as clear today as it was then, when I left them together in that little room.

I'd seen drunks before, but never anybody I knew. Except for papa, of course. But he left so long ago it hardly counts. When mama took me on the rounds of the houses she cleaned, before I was old enough to stay home and look after myself, I saw drunks. I saw people too helpless to get out of their chairs or pick themselves up from the hallways where they'd fallen. But I didn't know them. They belonged in other people's lives. They didn't touch me.

So, there I was that night, walking back in the rain to the tramstop saying never again. I was nineteen. I was about to be engaged, and I shouldn't have felt like I'd been sheltered all my life, but I did. I'd lived in a house full of women. With my sisters, with mama always looking after things because papa had walked out one Saturday morning and never come back. There I was, nineteen, and still feeling like a girl.

But I was determined as I walked back through the rain that I was never having any of that again. I'd rather stay at home, at mama's. I'd rather stay a mama's girl than grow up and drag him drunk from the gutter every pay day.

I told mama I wasn't going back and she said good riddance because she hated all drink. I told her I was gonna stay home, and she laughed and nodded her head. But as soon as I told her all this, I knew it wasn't true. I knew I'd already outgrown the house. And if I'd left anyone, if I'd left anywhere, I'd left home.

The phone calls came the next day, early in the morning, one after the other. But I expected them and I told mama I wasn't home to him. It rang again and again. Then it rang one time and I forgot that I wasn't in and picked the receiver up. Of course, it was him.

He was promising a whole new start. A clean sweep, he called it. I said no. He called back again. Then again. No more grog, he said. We'll move to the country when we're married, he said. Away from all the grog, the pubs and the boozers. And mama was standing in front of me, listening to me while I said no again. She was shaking her head, over and again, agreeing with every final 'no' that I uttered. We'll find a country town, he went on. Away from everybody. A clean start. A nice town, he said. Away from the city, he said again. With lots of country around it. And, somehow, I could imagine it. I knew it was mad, but I could see it. And it looked good. I was quiet as he talked. He knew he was onto something, so he went on and on about the country, and the more he went on and on about it the more I could see it. Then I nodded. I nodded my head, just the once. And I could hear the word 'yes' somewhere in the house, in the hall, dropping into place like a felt hat onto a stand. And mama was walking away wringing her hands.

It all happened in half a day, between a rainy night and a bright morning. That evening, a still one, with a cool winter tang in the air, I walked down Tivoli Street to meet him. The leaves were crunching under my feet and my eyes were wide open. I know they were. My strides were longer as I turned into Toorak Road, my steps were surer. I wasn't ready for any of it the previous night, but I was now. And what I couldn't tell mama, what I knew from the moment I woke up, with an ache in a part of my heart that had never been there before, was that something had begun and I was going to follow it through. I was going to follow it all through, whatever it came to.

The songs in all the movies had always told me it had to be love when it felt so right. That love was like dancing with the right partner. One step flowing naturally into the next. Forever. It wasn't quite like that, I knew as much by that night. But I also knew something was happening to me. For the movies also told me that love had a look, an unmistakable look, and I knew I had it, in my eyes and all over my face. There for everyone to see. And love had a sound too. And that sound was all around me that night. The tram bells played little jingles all along Toorak Road. I can still hear them. Even now, whenever a tram passes I hear the traces of those jingles. Poor me. Poor, silly bloody me. I had the look. I heard music in the traffic. And even though all my better voices told me that the song was lying, that it wasn't so right after all, that it was all wrong, and that the trams were just going clang-clang like they always did, I didn't listen. And if I had it all back I still wouldn't listen. I know I wouldn't. What else could I do?

It's then that she glances round at Vic as they walk along, notices the greying sides of his head, the grey temples of his trimmed curly hair, but for that moment she only remembers those dark curls as they once were. And Vic catches that look in her eyes, like he knows she's remembering the old days, and he gives her a snort of a laugh and looks out towards the pine trees of the school.

There she was, sitting up on the handlebars, legs either side of the wheel, not saying a word. And she was light. Like she wasn't sitting on the handlebars at all, but just above them. I felt no weight, no strain, no effort. I was pushing the bike up a hill into South Yarra. The street was clear and we rode down the middle of it in between the tram tracks. And she wasn't saying a word, I remember that. At one point she turned around and smiled, almost laughed, but most of the time she was just sitting there. Quiet. Looking down at the tracks between her legs.

I was gliding up the hill, past all the closed shops, like there was no hill at all. The road should have been slippery and difficult from the rain. It should have been an effort to peddle the bike, but I didn't feel a thing. She was sitting, staring down at the rails and I just knew she was smiling. I didn't even have to ask her. We'd just met at the Palais and I'd only known her a few hours, but I was sure. And even though it had only been a couple hours, I already felt like there was a before and an after. What I was when I rode down to the dance hall earlier that night was before. The ride home was after. In between I met Rita. And I was scared. Somewhere in me I was trembling. But where was it coming from? I did a mental search as we were riding along. It wasn't in my hands, not in my fingers, or my throat. Not in any place you could see. But where? And as I was peddling along, as the peddles went round and round, as we rolled over the railway bridge, past the station towards Chapel Street, I knew it was way down inside my best shoes. In a place so deep it wouldn't show.

The lights at Chapel Street didn't stop us. There was no one else on the road. We passed through the intersection and she went 'ooh' at the red light, then 'ooh' over her shoulder at me. And all the time I was asking myself the question: what do you do with a woman like this? What do you do? I was asking myself the question all along the street, as we left the intersection behind, and as we passed the gardens, the shops and the houses. I was asking myself the same question over and again because I'd never had a woman like her before. And then it hit me like an on-coming train. You marry her.

And when the answer hit me I could have sworn we'd stopped dead on the road. I could have sworn everything had stopped; the wind, the clouds, the moon. The whole show. But I looked down at the wheels of my bike and they were turning, down at the chain and the sockets and the pedals, and they were all moving. And then I looked down at my feet where I was trembling.

She raised her arm and pointed out her street. Home James, she said, and I was laughing. She was laughing. All along her street we were both laughing and I knew I was gone. You marry her, this voice was saying. You marry her. Nothing else for it. And when we finally stopped laughing and I slowed the bike at the front of that big, wide house of hers, I raised my head to the sky and took a good look at it. Then she handed me a slip of paper and disappeared through her door.

Vic is quiet. He has taken his wallet from his pocket and is flicking through its contents as if searching for the slip of paper Rita gave him that night, and the telephone number that was written on it. As if recovering that note, and looking at the scrawled telephone number, might recover the time itself.

It was the night his life turned. He knows that. It was the night he asked himself over and over the same question, what do you do? And it was the night he answered it. And when he realised that he'd really answered the question before he'd even asked it, he knew his old life was finished. Even though he'd always told himself, and everybody else had always told him too, that he'd be a fool to ever marry. He knew that even fools had their moment of truth, and this fool's moment had arrived.

16.

Smoothing the Rails

The air-conditioned dining car, with its imitation oak walls, is situated in the middle of the *Spirit*. The diners, seated at the tables, are watching the last of the summer sky dim. The train has reached the outer suburbs of the city and the diners can see the scattered weatherboard houses, the bare, flat yards, the dirt roads and the open paddocks of thistle and long grass. Soon the sky will be black and they will be staring at their own faces in the dining-car windows or in the windows of their compartments.

Throughout this time, while the first-class passengers are being served their meals in the dining car, they are only faintly aware of the gentle, rocking rhythm of the train and the steady clickety-clack of the wheels passing over the welded joints in the track. The ride is so smooth that nobody remarks upon it. The diners might even forget there is a driver at the front of the train. There are no sudden jolts, no bumps. And even when the train pulls into its scheduled stops later in the evening, the slowing of the train will barely be noticed.

And so too for the passengers in the second-class compartments who have either brought their meals with them or are munching on their railway pasties or sipping their railway tea. They watch the changing colour of the passing country, they chew thoughtfully on their tomato and onion sandwiches, and pour their tea from thermos to cup without ever remarking upon the ease of it all. From compartment to compartment, carriage to carriage, the smooth nature of the ride takes place without comment.

Paddy Ryan is leaning back in his seat chewing on a ham and mustard sandwich. The mug of tea beside him is still. The fireman remarks upon a Melbourne-bound goods, still an hour away. Paddy nods. When the time comes they will slow at the lights outside a large country town. This will allow the goods train time to slip into a loop. The *Spirit* will then continue on its journey and the goods will wait for Paddy to pass, before slipping out the other end of the loop and continuing on its journey through to Melbourne. It is a simple manoeuvre and Paddy thinks no more about it as he takes another bite from his sandwich.

The teaspoon rattles in the mug of tea beside him. Paddy makes the most minute of adjustments to the speed of the train and the spoon stops rattling. A hush falls over the cabin. The light has almost gone from the sky and the twin beams of the engine's headlights converge at a distant point on the tracks where a small flock of sheep runs from the approaching train to the shelter of a tree in a paddock.

17.

Papa

Of course mama never approved. She knew what I was getting myself into, she said again and again. She knew because she'd been there. As far as she was concerned I was just marrying my papa all over again, and I was a bloody fool if I couldn't see it. I pleaded with mama. I said that it would be different, that I wouldn't be living her life all over again. That I wasn't marrying papa. I nearly said that I never knew papa anyway, and that it was all her fault. But I didn't.

It was true, though. There was always mama, but no papa. And, I swear, there's not a day goes by when I don't remember the last of papa.

I was watching the sun coming through the screen door of the old home in Tivoli Street. It was a Saturday morning sun. Bright and warm in the heart of winter. I was sitting on the floor or standing in the hall watching. I don't remember. Papa was standing at the door with his hat and coat on, a newspaper in his hand. I could see a small overnight bag on the front porch and mama was nowhere in sight. Papa said he was just going down the street to see a man about a horse and that he'd be back soon. He bent down, kissed me on the cheek and gave me a small brown bag of broken biscuits.

I knew he wasn't just going down the street to see a man about a horse, and even now I can still hear the door creak, I still hear the groan of the old rusted springs. I still see papa picking up his bag from the porch and walking out along the garden path. He raised his old hat at the gate, smiled a big smile, his black moustache all turned up at the edges, his pipe hanging from the corner of his mouth, and then he was gone.

But I smelt pipe tobacco in the hallway all day. Long, sweet clouds of pipe smoke, slowly settling onto the furniture, the hat stand, the coat stand, the old chair, the shoe rack, the umbrellas, settling on it all, in the still hallway, long, sweet clouds of pipe smoke. And I followed it with my nose, out through the screen door like I was following papa's scent. Out into the garden, and I didn't even have to use my nose, I saw it with my eyes, a long, still trail of white smoke hanging over the garden path because there was no wind that day. It was Saturday morning, bright with sunshine, there was no wind and papa's trail was in front of me. I closed my eyes and followed it all the way to the front gate, until my hands hit the painted wire of the gate and I knew I couldn't go any further. I opened my eyes again, climbed up onto the gate and looked down the street, but there was no papa.

So I stood at the gate, swung back and forth and sucked broken biscuits from the brown bag that papa gave me. All the time I knew mama was somewhere back in the house, but she left me alone, let me stand at the gate all morning sucking on broken biscuits and waiting for papa. But when the day clouded over and the wind sprang up there was still no sign of papa. Even the sweet smell of his tobacco had gone from the garden now, and if I'd run out into the street and tried to follow his trail with my nose I couldn't have because there was no trail left. And so I waited, hanging over the front gate, till I'd finished sucking on the bag of biscuits and the afternoon turned grey.

Inside the house I could smell where papa had been; in the hallway, the lounge room, and the kitchen. And when I asked mama where papa was she said he'd gone visiting. He was visiting friends and he'd be back. But mama wasn't looking up from the kitchen table where she was rolling pastry and I knew she was lying. And although I knew I'd go on waiting at the front looking for papa in the street, I also knew there was no point.

But one day, a lot later, mama, my sisters and me were all walking down Chapel Street on a Sunday afternoon, in our best walking clothes. Everybody in the street was in their Sunday best, with their hats and gloves, and suddenly there was papa. On the other side of the street. And I said mama, there's papa, and I couldn't believe my eyes. He was walking along with a well-dressed woman and she was holding onto his arm, but I barely noticed her because I was watching papa. And once again I said, mama there's papa, but mama grabbed me by the arm and told me to shut up. She told everybody to join hands and look the other way and ignore papa.

I was looking across to the other side of the street while mama was dragging me along by the hand. Papa was raising his hat, waving at me with it and I waved back with my free hand. He was smiling that big smile, with his black moustache curled up at the corners. He blew a small, white cloud into the air, took his pipe from his mouth as he waved again, and I swear, from the other side of the street, over the cars and the trams, I could smell papa's sweet breath. Then we turned a corner into a small street.

It was the last time I saw papa, and I never knew why we weren't allowed to stop and talk to him. It's not fair what people keep to themselves, what they keep from you, because when they die they take it with them.

And I swear, I'm certain, that if I ever leave, if I ever go, Michael will know why. He will be told what happened, and he will know why people drift apart and leave each other, and he won't spend the rest of his life wondering why. He won't spend the rest of his life trying to understand something he knows he never can, because everybody who could possibly tell him what happened is dead.

18.

Ten Lousy Shillings

His father's wallet contained an odd collection of bits and pieces. There was never much money there, for Michael had flicked through it on a number of occasions. Sometimes it was filled more with scraps of paper that had bits of poetry written on them than anything else. Something his father had read, something he'd heard somewhere, something that impressed him enough to want to write it down and carry with him. There was, in fact, a line of poetry he felt sure was in his wallet. They had been talking earlier to the Millers about the sky and Vic had been about to catch that sky for all of them with a line of poetry, the way he liked to. But the poetry had suddenly deserted him and the line wasn't in his wallet when he went to look for it. He could have sworn he'd written it down. But no. There were trees, rivers, bullocks, beaches, mountain ranges, towns, trains and strange birds in that wallet, but no skies. Even now as they walk along the street he examines the wallet, puzzled as to where the line might be and even tries to remember it. But the moment for it has passed. Michael watches as his father returns the wallet to his trouser pocket, along with the cork-tipped cigarettes and the lighter.

Three of them. There were only three of them. There always seemed to be more than three. But one day Michael numbered the members of the family and was shocked to discover that there were, in fact, only three. No more. He'd never looked at it like that before, and suddenly three was a small number. The house, with its radio, and dishes and talk makes them large. But the arithmetic is true. They are only three. And sometimes, when his mother's work takes her away, they are only two. Then, when the house is empty at night, one. There always seemed to be more than there are, but suddenly one is never far away.

Michael had waited up most of the night by himself. He knew the pattern. His mother went to the country for a week working, his father got drunk. His mother called in the evenings and asked if everything was fine and Michael always said it was. She would ask again and he would tell her once more that everything was fine.

It was late, damp and cold. The lawn was sodden and the plum tree at the back was sagging under the weight of the night's rain. Then there was a sudden clatter, a tumbling, falling sound like the briquettes being delivered and his father was home.

He was slumped up against the wall, sitting on a foldout garden lounge, when Michael stepped from the kitchen into the closed-in porch. Vic looked up and nodded, Michael just stood there, studying his father, deciding there and then that if his father was too drunk to get himself to bed then he could just sleep on the banana lounge. He asked Michael if he'd had dinner and he said yes.

'What did you have?'

'Chops.'

'Were they good?'

Michael shrugged his shoulders as if to say they were chops.

Vic nodded, the lower half of his jaw falling away slightly from the upper half. He was staring at the wall. His wallet was open on his lap, his pay packet beside that.

'Let me explain something.' He held up a handful of pound notes. 'A little lesson.'

Michael had heard it all before and wasn't

interested. His father continued, still holding up the handful of notes. 'That's the mortgage, on this place.' He looked about the porch shaking his head then put the money to one side. 'And this,' he held up more notes, 'is your school.'

Gradually, he moved all the notes from his pay packet to the other side of his lap, itemising each one as he went, until he was left with a single ten shilling note and some small change.

He shifted on the banana lounge and watched pound notes and silver coins fall to the floor. But he kept the ten shilling note in his hand and held it up to Michael. 'And this. This is what I'm left with. I'm up in the middle of the night driving those filthy bloody engines for this?'

Michael nodded, knowing exactly what was coming next. Vic knew he'd heard it all before and could see the bored look on Michael's face, but continued all the same.

'This is what happens when you get a house and a family. You wind up with ten lousy shillings. Never get a house and a family. Stay free.'

He looked for a reaction from Michael, but he only nodded. Vic then leaned his head back against the wall and gave a slight grunt through his nose, the stale smell of the night's beer coming from his nostrils.

Michael watched him, knowing that he would be asleep soon and that he'd be impossible to move.

'You should go to bed, before you fall asleep.'

'Did your mother call?'

'Yes.'

'What did you tell her?'

'I told her everything was fine.'

His father nodded and turned silent.

'You shouldn't stay here,' Michael said, leaning against the flyscreen kitchen door.

'You go,' his father's eyes opened slightly, registering his child's disapproval. 'You go. I'll just sit here for a while.' His eyes remained momentarily clear as he stared at Michael. 'You must learn', he added, with the sudden clarity and precision of a sober man, mindful of the judgement in Michael's eyes, 'you must learn to respect my weakness.'

He closed his eyes again, his kitbag, his notes, his coins at his feet on the floor. Then, slowly, Vic rolled to one side and lay down on the plastic banana lounge. Michael wavered near the kitchen door, deciding whether to speak again. He left and returned with a blanket, with which he covered the sleeping figure of his father. He then gathered the scattered money up from the floor and put it all back inside the pay packet; the pound notes, the silver coins, the copper coins, and the ten lousy shillings.

Michael made sure the back door was locked, turned the porch light out, and closed the kitchen door slowly, so as not to make a noise. In the bathroom he brushed his teeth and prepared for sleep. The toothbrush and the running water, the only sounds in the house. He calculated the days of the week remaining. It was Wednesday. The next day was Thursday. Soon, soon the week would be over and they would number three again.

Later, in his room, he mulled over the night. Noting how the moods change, from day to day, from week to week. Some days, after the drunken pay nights, it takes all his father has just to drag himself to work and face those filthy bloody engines again, and he can't wait to be finished with them and let somebody else take over. On these days he always told Michael never to drive engines. To leave trains to mugs like him who were good for nothing else. But Christ, he would add, Christ we can drive those bloody things.

Other days, like a warm afternoon the previous week, he would be happy. No more talk of filthy engines, that day he was pleased to be going to work. He had a good train, good weather and a good shift. Just like it would always be when he finally joined the Big Wheel. It was at times like these when he was at his happiest, when he was preparing for work.

Michael recalled the day clearly, in all its detail, because he had never thought about his father as being anything other than his father. That was all that was needed. But as he recalled that day he saw, once again, his father sitting on a small stool in the laundry at the back of the house. It was where he kept his bag, his swabs, his soaps, his manuals, his work coat and overalls. And for this reason the laundry, for Michael, always had the smell of soap, cinders, tea and steam. Especially, the smell of steam. It was a smell that told a story in itself for it brought the job into the house. The overalls that hung from hangers, the blue cotton caps, and the open leather bag, a Gladstone, filled the room with the smell of completed shifts, with the residual particles of those days and nights when things went well and they'd steam through warm nights into brilliant summer sunrises while the towns and suburbs slept, when the engine would drive itself and Vic would be doing the thing he does best with such ease that his mind was barely conscious of the little tasks he was constantly performing and there was only a moment's distance between driving through the country and arriving at the city yards. Or they brought with them reminders of when things went badly, of when they sat in country sidings for hours waiting for engine parts to arrive, drinking tea and Vic swearing all the time that he'd leave those filthy engines the first chance he got.

But on this particular afternoon his father was happy. Michael stood in the doorway watching as his father polished his work boots. And it was then he realised that the picture he saw of his father at that moment, was a complete one. There, on the small stool in the laundry at the back of the house, polishing his boots and preparing for the work he does best, was somebody who lacked nothing and asked for nothing. He was happy.

And it was then that Michael, calmly and matter-of-factly, told his father that he couldn't imagine him doing anything else. That he couldn't imagine him being anything other than an engine driver. And his father paused from polishing his boots and looked up with a broad smile across his face and nodded to Michael as if greeting a friend. They were both silent then and Michael leaned against the door while his father completed the task of polishing his boots. Michael didn't tell his father that he didn't think much of engines himself. He didn't tell him that that was his father's world, not his, and never would be. Besides, you didn't get a girl like Patsy Bedser driving engines.

Years afterwards, when Michael thought of his father, he would see him packing his work bag then carrying it up their street, with a hunch and a lean to his stride, as he walked to work. And that would always define him.

He would always be striding away. Just out of reach. A big smile, a big laugh, and a big flourishing wave of a big hand before striding away. A walk that knows only one direction. And always just out of reach – this night, as they walk along their street to the Englishman's, and years later, after he had died in a one-bedroom flat in Tweed Heads at three or four in the morning with no one else around him to whom he could give one last big smile or one last flourishing wave of a big hand, before striding away forever.

By then his possessions – a few shirts, a good pair of trousers, his everyday shorts, the white, knee-high socks he wore on the golf course and his leather sandals – would all fit into a couple of black plastic garbage bags. A box of his books, among them titles like *Take Me To Russia*, which at this moment sits on the bookshelves in the lounge room, will eventually find their way into Michael's possession, along with a Larry Adler Professional 16 chromatic harmonica. The golf clubs that he won in a raffle after buying all the tickets because he didn't have the heart to lump them onto his mates, will travel down to Melbourne a week after his funeral, ferried overnight in the luggage van of the *Spirit*. The garbage bags will disappear into the back of a van, the books will wait with the caretaker, and the old-furnished, one-bedroom flat will be cleared and cleaned in the one day, ready for a new occupant.

And that's the way his life will end. A quiet funeral. Rita, Michael, and a few of those sympathetic strangers he would call friends throughout those last years. A couple of drinks afterwards. A short drive to the cemetery. And a nice spot in a tropical garden for the urn full of dust that he will become.

But none of this has happened. Not yet. The suburban sky still contains the last of its peach glow. And that spring morning in late October, that dark hour, estimated by the coroner at being around three or four o'clock, when he would wake in enormous pain and know that his time was up, is still years away. And Vic and Rita are still strolling along their street ahead of Michael, both oblivious of whatever it is they may be in for.

Michael stops in his tracks a moment and watches them. His mother rests her hand on her father's arm. She is asking him a question. His father snorts into laughter. They look almost happy. Maybe tonight they are. Even at this age Michael knows that his father should never have married. But he did. And now the three of them are walking down their street on a Saturday night to an engagement party. Soon somebody else will be married.

His mother's hand falls from his father's arm, her fingers slide down his shoulder slowly, stopping at his forearm where his shirt is rolled, staying there for a moment, like they don't want to leave. Yes, Michael decides, tonight they are happy. And he is happy. His right arm rolls quickly over as he hurls another imaginary ball into the night. Another, faster than the one before. And another, faster still. Perhaps they won't leave each other, after all. Perhaps they'll stay. And what he heard the week before as his parents were sitting in the kitchen and he was standing at his bedroom door was just talk.

19.

Don't be Cruel

The car drew into the siding in front of the church, like it had throughout most of that winter and spring. The car knew its way by then. It must have, for often she had no memory of the drive, so familiar was the landscape that she failed to notice it. As she stepped into the doorway, and as the door closed behind her, she was aware of leaving behind all the things that were familiar to her. Every time it was the same sensation, the same thrill, the same fear that she may never return to it.

But not that day. Patsy had come to a decision. And she'd come to tell Jimmy. Jimmy. The hi-fi salesman with the long legs and the cowboy lope. All through the winter and the spring, when her work shifts made it possible, they'd met here. But it was always going to end. Her plumber had proposed to her through the week and she found herself saying yes.

Jimmy's fun, but there's no guarantee, no future in Jimmy. And so she arrived early and wandered about the church working out just what she was going to say. Because Jimmy wouldn't like this. She worked out all sorts of ways of saying it. Understanding ways. Matter-of-fact ways. Sad ways. But Jimmy had no sooner than arrived and she blurted it out. All of it, right down to the summer engagement party.

At first he laughed, thinking it was a joke. But she wasn't laughing. With his hands on his hips he looked down at his black, pointed boots and slowly shook his head from side to side. Then he eyeballed her. Thanks for giving it to me gently he said, and looked at his watch. It was only a minute or so ago that he had stepped in the door. He walked around the old church a bit, stamping his heels on the floor with his hands on his hips and sighing. He was cranky. She could see that. She didn't say a word, didn't move. She let him wander around. He stopped every now and then as if he was about to say something, but he shook his head instead, and stared intently at a flock of stained-glass sheep.

He asked her if it was final and he could tell from the way she answered that it was. He looked at the sheep again and nodded to himself. That was when he casually turned around to her and suggested they had plenty of time for one last root before they went their separate ways. One last what? she asked. That was when his voice changed and all the crankiness started coming out his mouth in a rush. One last root, he said, louder. That's what we've been doing all winter, he yelled. We've been coming here and rooting each other. Or don't you like the sound of that?

She knew why he'd said it. So they could have a fight. So he could blow his top, call her a dumb slag and be the first one to leave. But she didn't give him the chance and she was out the door before he could start up again.

He followed her and outside he was shaking his right hand at her and telling her she was a fool. She kept walking. He kept following her. His voice was louder, loud enough to disturb the birds in the trees. She was worse than a fool by then, she was a dumb bitch, and a lousy root anyway. Just like all the other dumb bitches around the place. That was when he called her a slag as well and she shook her head because she knew it had been coming all along. But by the time she reached the Morris he'd blown off a bit of steam and was leaning over the open car door, asking her to stay. She said no. He asked her again. She shook her head. And that was when he said please and kicked the car tyre. He was still talking when she started the engine. She heard the word please again, quieter this time. His voice wobbled. He could almost have been singing. And she knew then that he called her a root to hurt her the same way she'd just hurt him. She knew she meant more than that to him and wished she didn't. Almost wished she was just some dumb root he'd met along the way. Then nobody would get hurt. But if she were she'd probably be stupid enough to fall in love, and then she'd be the one saying please and Jimmy would be doing exactly what she's doing now.

She might have started crying at this stage or later on during the drive back. She was never really sure, but she shook her head one last time and left Jimmy standing there. That was it. Afterwards, whenever she played a record on the hi-fi she'd see the reflection of Jimmy in her rear-vision mirror and hear his last please being blown away in the dust.

But part of her always knew that it was going to take more than a cloud of dust to blow Jimmy away. One day, one night, he'd be there again in front of her, brushing the road off him and singing something about a teddy bear.

20.

The Endless Sky

The sky is darkening. Michael spots the comet, the stars gradually assembling around it, and he walks along with his eyes turned upwards. He knows the street will end somewhere in the thickening light ahead of him. Beyond that the schoolyard ends, and the old wheat road beyond that. The suburb itself ends where the houses give way to Scotch thistles and open paddocks. Even the open paddocks end. But not the sky.

Paddocks eventually run into deserts, or forest, or cliffs and simply fall into the sea. But look to the sky in any direction and it never stops. Michael swivels on his heels, completes a full circle while still looking up, taking in the dying peach glow as he does. All of it, in whatever direction the full circle has him facing, continuing forever.

His parents, who have moved ahead of Michael again, turn to catch the spectacle of their child spinning on the spot again and again, with his face up to the sky. He is on the point of losing his balance, of staggering off the footpath and onto the road, when his mother calls out and he stops in mid-circle.

'What are you looking at?' she asks. And he tells her he is looking at the sky. 'What part of the sky?'

'The part I'm standing under. It goes on forever,' he says, keeping his eyes on the heavens and not looking at his parents, now stationary and standing side by side on the footpath. 'Have you thought of that?'

His father snorts with low laughter.

'It's best not to think about that.'

'Why?' Michael's eyes suddenly drop from the sky to his father, puzzled.

'Because you'll go mad,' his father says, as he turns and resumes walking up the street.

Why mad? Michael asks himself, now back to earth. Why mad? He likes the idea of at least something in this world going on forever. His parents are now slowly walking on ahead, talking quietly. He can't hear the words from where he stands. They are talking the same way they did that night a week before, when they sat up in the kitchen talking well into the night. Every now and then Michael could hear what they said. They talked about the end of things; of the house, of the three of them living in the house together. The end of all the usual mornings and evenings, dinners and lunches. Until then the end of it all was as inconceivable as a sky that eventually came to an end. It couldn't happen.

He wasn't meant to hear, but he could. He was standing by his door and he could make out the quiet, confidential voices of his parents in the kitchen. It was after ten and the light from under the kitchen door fanned the carpet.

There were long silences, the occasional sound of a spoon in a cup, the shuffling of a chair over the lino floor. They weren't fighting and Michael could tell from their measured and quiet manner of speaking, that it was an important conversation.

The night before had been bad. His mother had waited at home, dressed to go out, but his father had been late from work and too drunk to go anywhere. He had fallen over onto the lounge-room floor and lay there listening to her insults and her rage with the occasional raising of his eyebrows. He knew it was coming and he didn't care. She could say what she liked and it wouldn't matter. Eventually, having exhausted her anger, his mother had given up. It was pointless and she had left him there to sleep on the floor.

They were talking quietly in the kitchen, and as Michael opened his bedroom door further still he could hear his mother's voice.

'If you can't promise,' and Michael waited for his mother to finish the sentence. 'If you can't promise, then there's nothing left for it. We may as well sell everything. Sell the house, start all over again. I'm not going through another summer like this. I'm not going through another night like that.' And from the opened door of his room Michael could imagine his mother pointing to the lounge room as she spoke.

She stopped then and Michael knew she was waiting for his father to speak. There was silence.

'Well?'

Suddenly a chair was shifted, scraping the floor, and Michael quickly closed his bedroom door and stepped back into the darkness of his room as the kitchen door opened and his mother walked up the hallway to their bedroom.

As she passed he heard the words 'No more', then 'Never again'. He sat on the edge of his bed in the dark and waited for his mother to return to the kitchen. When she did, she closed the door softly so that, he realised, they wouldn't disturb his sleep. But he wasn't sleeping. He was sitting on the edge of his bed in the darkness of his room, listening to the quiet, confidential voices of his mother and father.

And although he could no longer hear the words, he knew now what they were talking about.

Michael has ceased turning round in circles and is standing still on the dirt footpath watching his parents walking away from him along the street. He is waiting till they turn and acknowledge his absence. But they don't turn and they don't even notice that he's not there with them. In a panic, he suddenly runs along the footpath and catches his parents just as they turn around to him. He takes both their hands for a moment, then swings from their elbows and catapults himself forward, into the air and onto the path in front of them. The three walk on in silence towards the Bedser's, the music from the hi-fi now calling out to them in the clear night air.

21.

Mr Van Rijn

Peter Van Rijn is closing his car door and is no sooner behind the wheel than he is backing out of the driveway and onto the dirt road, which he stirs into a dusty cloud as he accelerates towards his shop, passing a slow procession of families as he goes. At the bottom of the street he passes George Bedser's house, where the party lights are glowing in the twilight, temporarily transforming it into a river barge, floating on the long, khaki grasses of the vacant lots either side of it. He turns left, then right, and takes the old wheat road to his shop.

When television first came to the suburb it was Peter Van Rijn who sold them. He grew up in Delft, in a house by the river, not far from the cathedral. A print of Vermeer's *View Of Delft* hangs in his workshop. An electrical engineer, he spends his working hours repairing the worn parts of wireless sets, replacing old valves and soldering broken wires back together so that the wireless will function again and his customers will be able to hear their music, their cricket and their news.

But it was television that made him. At first his shop window was filled with wirelesses, transistors and record players, with large colour posters on the walls advertising the latest European and American gramophones. When television arrived, however, his shop window changed. The radios, transistors and record players made way for television sets, the screens of which would all be aimed at the shop window so as to catch the eyes of the people passing. It is still his weekday practice to switch one of the televisions on, between five and seven o'clock, and commuters walking home from work often pause to watch the new American serials or the old movie cartoons. On Saturday nights he leaves the television on until transmission ceases.

It was an act of generosity and an astute strategy, for it not only allowed people to watch the televisions free of charge, it also gave them a taste for television, making the lounge room and the wireless dull by comparison when they returned home. In summer, families would go to Peter Van Rijn's shop window as they would to the cinema.

There, they would stand about on the footpath watching whatever came on. In time he sold all his televisions. And as soon as they were sold he got more. For a short time televisions transformed his shop, from a quiet radio repairer's to the most successful business in the street. But not everybody was happy.

He parks his car at the front, jumps from the driver's seat, and stands running his fingers through his dark, curly hair. The glass from his shop window is all over the footpath, and while occasional shards are still wedged inside the window frame, most of the window has been shattered and the glass is either inside or outside the shop. Remarkably, as he steps forward and peers into the window, nothing has been stolen or damaged; all the televisions, radios, gramophones and transistors are exactly where they were placed. It is only when he has finished counting the items and stock in the window that he looks to the tiles below it and sees in large, red print the word 'commie'.

A young man, with a young family, who left Holland after the war with the precise intention of leaving all this hatred behind, he spends the next hour sweeping the glass from the footpath and taking all the stock from the window, placing it in the back workroom which he can lock. When he is finished he takes a bucket and scrubbing brush and removes the painted word from the tiles at the front of the shop. Finally, he pastes large pieces of cardboard across the broken window and returns to his car.

There he sits for a long time, quietly listening to the car radio. The shop has taken years of patient work to build up. He is proud of the way the shop looks, proud of the up-to-date goods he has for sale. He keeps in constant touch with all the latest trends in his business. If, he has always argued to himself, he feels good about walking into his shop, his customers will feel good about it as well, for a shop should feel good to be in. He is proud of his displays, of his posters, and of his new cataloguing system which tells him at a glance where everything is, as well as the dates of ordering, purchasing and selling.

Occasionally people pass and pause at the now taped-up window, and he is glad that the crudely painted word has been removed. As he sits in the car he takes gum from the glove box and silently chews on it while watching the street, the shattered window of his shop looking like the shattered windows in all the bombed-out streets he left behind, and at the occasional strollers who may even have made a special trip to stand at his window. He feels responsible for their disappointment. Some of these families walk over a mile, there and back, for the Saturday-night treat of standing at his window and watching the television they can't afford to buy. Before starting the car again he rests his chin on the steering wheel, taps the dashboard lightly with his fingers, then turns the ignition.

As he drives slowly back along the old wheat road, past the Presbyterian church on his left, past the school, and into his street, he notes the muted lights of the quiet houses and the bare front yards in which modest gardens are struggling to grow. That afternoon, as he drove home in the late, summer sun, the scene had been a pleasant, reassuring one. Now, he passes those quiet houses oppressed by the uneasy thought that any one of them could have thrown the brick.

As he pulls back into his driveway he nods, without smiling, to a family on the footpath opposite his house. They wave back and he parks the car, then walks inside to change for the party.

Michael waves as the old, black Vauxhall belonging to Mr Van Rijn comes to a stop in his driveway. Michael is one of those who, after school, have often lingered at his shop window for over an hour watching the cartoons. When Mr Van Rijn is gone Michael returns his attention to his parents and the rest of the street. He slowly walks backwards, deliberately facing the direction from which they have come.

The lights in Peter Van Rijn's lounge room snap on. The window is open. Van Rijn's voice is low, but his wife is clearly proclaiming, as if to the whole street, that no, she will not go to the party. She will not mix with people who could do this. And nor should he. The window shuts like a guillotine. Their voices are lost and Michael turns back towards his parents.

A summer song is just audible. It carries from the Bedser's lounge room along the street to Vic, Rita and Michael. The song is familiar, and although the words aren't clear, Vic sings them in silent accompaniment. It is this year's summer song. Every year has a summer song, and this one talks of soda and drive-ins and pretzels and beer.

But even as he hums the tune to himself a steam engine passes over the high trestle bridge in the Scotch thistle country just to the north of the suburb. Vic closes his eyes and turns his right ear to the sound and listens like a blind man. The sound is faint, but he knows it's steam. He knows the rhythm, the chug of a steam engine, and there are moments, his nose to the breeze, when he swears he can almost smell the thing.

22.

The Art of Engine Driving

The art of locomotive engine driving can only be acquired after years of study, patient practice and experience.

Bagley's Australian Locomotive Engine Drivers'
Guide

Somewhere out there they are making fire. A man, his face smudged black from dust and cinders, is standing legs astride the footplate to steady himself at high speed and he is carrying coals, broken into small pieces for even burning, from the tender to the furnace. The door of the furnace will be open and its glow will light the cabin, and the coals will fall gold and vermilion from the shovel into the furnace to make fire. And from the fire will come steam, and from the steam will come power. What is a locomotive engine? this man will, like all firemen, be asked at his driver's examination. Vic poses the question to himself as he listens to the train cross the trestle bridge and answers as he did years before. And the answer comes as automatically now as it did then. What is a locomotive engine? A steam engine placed on wheels capable of producing motive power to propel itself and draw carriages on a railway. And that is what the man with the shovel in his hand is doing when he makes fire. He is creating motive power, somewhere out there in the thistle country to the north of the suburb where the trestle bridge spans a wide, ancient river valley.

To stand on the footplate with Paddy Ryan was to stand in the studio of a great artist, for Paddy Ryan was acknowledged as the Michelangelo of engine drivers.

The engine cabin was his classroom. And whatever engine they drove, it was always the same; a furnace fired in just the right way, the smell of steam, burning coal and freshly brewed tea, and all the instruments and gauges cleaned and polished well before the drive. In this way both fire and instruments glowed, night or day, winter or summer, and Paddy's cabins always had the stamp of a master. Work was never work, nothing was ever ordinary, and the seven years that Vic spent learning the trade as Paddy's fireman always felt like a privilege. Even the impromptu lessons he conducted, in question and answer, remained as vivid as when they were spoken.

The drivers' classes at the Institute told him all he could learn from books and diagrams, but it was Paddy Ryan who took him over the steam engine, piece by piece, as if it were his own private invention. Paddy who taught him the importance of a clean cabin in which to work. And it was Paddy who taught the twenty-year-old Vic all he would ever need to know about the Westinghouse brake, the pistons and the boiler, who broke it all down into its constituent parts in so clear and simple a way as to ensure that Vic knew their mechanics better than he knew the workings of his own heart, lungs and legs. It was Paddy who taught Vic how to fire an engine up, how to lay the coals out so they glowed even and hot for the longest possible time, how to use the sand on rainy mornings so that the wheels wouldn't slip and spin uselessly on the tracks, Paddy who taught him how to ride the curves, who taught him not to be afraid of speed, and not to love it – but how to use it. How to stop a train without snapping it in half, and how to pull into a station without taking the platform and everything else with him. And Paddy who taught him how to listen to an engine, to its beats and rhythms, to the point where presence of mind became absence of body.

To feel you were performing one, single, pure activity as well as it could be performed, to know something that thoroughly – that, to Vic, was almost the whole point of living, to find what you did best and then do it. That was the dream, and in the classroom of Paddy's cabin, the dream always felt near enough to be lived.

Paddy taught him all this. But he never taught Vic the tricks he learnt for himself. The ones that weren't in the books. Paddy never taught Vic how to smooth the rails, and Vic never learnt the art, not the way Paddy knew it. And not only because it was a mystery to Paddy himself, but because that was Paddy's signature. And it was always understood that Vic would have to find his own.

It was also Paddy who taught the young Vic how to drink. And for this reason and this reason alone, Paddy's name was always mud with Rita and she never allows him in the house.

Just as it was a privilege to stand on the footplate with Paddy, it was a privilege to stand at the public bar with him. And when Paddy suggested a drink at The Railway, you didn't hang about.

23.

The Six O'clock Swill

We are the parade of the rubber men. And we know it. Don't ever imagine that we're not so drunk we don't know we are. We hit the pub, The Railway, just near the yards, at five o'clock when the shift finishes and walk through the door into the roar of all the talk and the transistors, into the smoke, everybody either throwing them down or at the bar with their empty glasses plonked on the counter for quick service because every minute is precious. We walk through the door with legs beneath us and we leave an hour later with limbs of rubber.

We are ridiculous. We are a joke, and we know it. When time's up they throw us out into the street. And by quarter past six we're all trying to find a part of the footpath that's not moving beneath us. And when we do, we stay there for a while, till everything stops shifting about. Or we're propped up against the walls of the pub, or having a leak into the laneways, or spewing up into the gutters. We're not a pretty sight, and we know that too.

Out on the street we say our goodbyes, and we try to say all we've got to say to each other then, because nobody gets a chance to say all that much inside when you're pouring beers down your throat every five minutes. And besides, nobody can hear a word unless you're screaming into someone's ear, because everybody else is shouting at the bar for service. And then, before we know it, we're out on the streets and they're hosing down the floors inside the pub like it's a zoo or something, hosing and sweeping out the muck that we tramped in with us as well as the dirt and the cigarette butts and the spilt beer that we left behind. And sometimes we're standing out on the footpath, trying to finish the talk we never got the chance to finish inside, when the butts and the beer suddenly wash up around our feet and over our shoes, and we start to feel like we too have been hosed out into the street with the rubbish.

But when all the talk's finally out of the way, and we've said our see-you-laters, we start thinking about getting along. That's when we lift those rubber legs of ours. We start to move and the parade begins. Legs that knew only too well how to walk just an hour before have suddenly lost the talent for it. They quiver like jelly beneath us, and each leg has a different sense of direction. And, of course, waving goodbye and walking at the same time becomes a little tricky. But we give it a go and somehow manage to convince ourselves that it's all performed with the natural ease of just anybody heading home from work. But we know it's not. We know it's a fuck up. For there is a part of us that is always watching, watching from somewhere down at the back of the brain. And it's always there, shaking its head at this once functional body making a spectacle of itself. Every night the rubber army of the six o'clock swill, our bags clinking with the bottles we bought for the return journey, is back on the street. Swaying on the corners or tumbling into train carriages that will rock us to sleep and leave us snoring and breathing the last hour's drinking into the closed carriage for everyone to share.

And when we leave our trains and are standing back on the platforms of our stations, we begin the final march home. In the winter dark nobody sees us as we disappear, one by one, into our suburbs and streets and driveways. But in summer, that final rubber walk is performed in the full glare of the late-afternoon sun.

In his mind, Vic is leaving the station after one of the numerous sessions at The Railway and taking that final walk home, like he has so many times before. Like he did the previous week. As he approaches the Englishman's house he remembers the spectacle with sober detachment. The Gladstone bag that he carries is filled with swabs, soap, a tea jar, his billy, and the two bottles of Melbourne Bitter he bought at the pub. His folded newspaper sits on top. He has been drinking with his mates after work, and they have been drinking the only way they know how.

The sun is low across the flour mills and the shadows are long as he walks down the pathway that leads from the station to the old wheat road. As he crosses the road, passing the milk bar on one side and the television repairer's on the other, his head is still filled with the noise, the shouting, the radio, the races, the smells, the smoke and the arguments of that crowded hour in the pub. That crowded hour in which they all drink the only way they know how.

And, swaying as he moves, possibly shaking his head at something that may have been said, he turns into the old wheat road and walks home the only way he knows how, leaning into the street, leaning into the summer breeze as if warily advancing into a future that might shut down any minute and leave him stranded in the street. Dazed and staggering. Ridiculous again.

24.

Mr Malek

As they leave the house of Mr Van Rijn behind them they hear a voice, soft, but grumbling and argumentative. All three, Vic, Rita and Michael, suddenly swing round to the source of the sound. Standing at his front gate, in his best suit, tie and shined black shoes, is the short, square figure of Mr Malek. He is drunk already, muttering at his front gate and swaying from side to side, but he is not talking to anybody in particular. He is drunk on the clear liquid that he makes himself in his back yard.

His hands grip the iron gate as he leans forward, staring down to the dirt pathway, muttering something indistinct, possibly arguing with himself or with an invisible presence. The three of them try not to stare at the Polish gentleman swaying by his gate and carrying on an argument with increasing passion. He is repeating the same phrase over and again, and the three have slowed discernibly in their pace, concentrating now on what he is saying. At first it is utterly foreign. It could be German, an old Polish phrase or something in Russian. A place, a name. It is difficult to tell. Then he rattles his gate, raises his voice and everybody hears.

'Get fucked,' he says, rattling the gate again, but more furiously this time. 'Get fucked.'

Michael begins to laugh, but his mother stops him. Quiet, she says. Let him be. And in that still, soft summer night Mr Malek rattles the gate again and again, as if shaking the life out of somebody. The shaking increases and the rattling of the gate can now be heard all along the street, and all the families walking up the dirt footpath to the Englishman's house now turn to observe the spectacle of old man Malek, who is staring down at his feet in that deeply, private world he inhabits, shaking the life out of his front gate, oblivious of the street. He speaks little English and nobody really knows him. Any of the stories the street tells could be true, that he was a resistance fighter in the war, that he was captured and his mind went funny. That he was just a potato farmer who went broke and whose mind was always funny. That he lost his memory when a bomb went off and now he doesn't know who or where he is. The street believes the first story, is used to the sight of old man Malek rattling his front gate and lets him be.

His voice rises with the racket he is making and is now clearly audible to everybody.

'Get fucked,' he calls. 'I know what get fucked is. You think I don't know what get fucked is. I know it. You get fucked,' he suddenly calls, raising his head to the sky, amid a spasm of gate rattling, as if addressing himself to the setting sun or some face in the low, streaked cloud above the pine trees of the school.

Then just as suddenly he drops his head, the rattling of the gate slowly subsides, and his address returns to mutterings.

'And you. And you,' he says, nodding back down to the footpath now. Almost inaudibly, he adds, 'Everybody, get fucked.'

In his best clothes, he is dressed for the party, and like everybody else in the street he will have been invited. But he is already a tired figure. Silent now, with his elbows leaning on the gate, he is staring down at his shoes, shining in the twilight. He swivels his feet, from his heels, moving them backward and forward in an arc. He is almost dancing. His shoes swing from side to side, reflecting as they move the last of the sky's peach glow.

Soon, he turns those shoes around, faces his house, and takes the small stone pathway back up to his front door. It is early in the evening but he is already exhausted. He is stooped and every now and then there is a slight stagger, a stalling in his progress, a swaying from side to side as he negotiates the pathway.

Those families who are out in the street and who have been observing old man Malek's antics, now turn back to their conversations. Malek stops halfway along the path to his porch. He raises his hand to his chin, suddenly lost in thought and turns back to the street as if he really might join that pilgrimage down to the Englishman's house at the bottom of the street. Why not? The invitation is on his mantelpiece, he is invited after all. His suit and shirt are pressed and his shoes are luminous from having been polished all afternoon. Why not? But he suddenly drops his hand to his side, as if dropping the thought as well, and walks back to the house.

Inside he stands before the mantelpiece with the invitation to the engagement in his hands. He runs his fingers over the gold embossed card, then puts it back. The walls of the room are lined with photographs from another time and place, all family shots or country scenes. Through the lounge-room door his wife, dressed in her everyday clothes, looks up from the kitchen table and stares at him. She watched him polish his shoes that afternoon in readiness for the party. And when he asked her, she pressed his shirt and his suit. She even watched him dress, knotting and re-knotting his tie until it sat just right, and she started to believe that he really might go to this engagement after all. Then she watched him sit down to drink in his good suit and shoes and she knew he wasn't going anywhere.

She studies him, swaying before the mantelpiece with the invitation in his hand, says nothing, then returns to her task. She is making doughnuts. Rich European doughnuts, with four eggs and butter. Later, when they are ready, she will take them to the party and offer the plate to the Englishman as a gift for his daughter's engagement, but she will not stay.

As she stirs the mixture she tells her husband, in Polish, to sit down before he falls down. Old man Malek slumps into an armchair and loosens his tie. It may yet be early in the evening, and he may well have been dressed for the party since late in the afternoon, but he will be asleep in his armchair before it has begun.

While he is sleeping his wife will place his good shoes on the wooden rack in the bedroom before slipping out into the warm, summer air and delivering the gift of her plate. And when they ask her to join the party, she will thank them without speaking, shake her head, clasp her hands together, and hurry back into the warm scented air of the street.

At home she will stir old man Malek from his armchair and guide him to bed. When the house is cleaned, she will join him. She will lie there, unable to sleep, listening to the faint sounds of the gramophone music coming from the party, and the occasional bursts of laughter and cheers.

25.

Diesel and Steam

T he *Spirit* is now two hours away from the city and is nearing a station. Paddy knows the town, not just because he has driven there hundreds of times, but because Vic once lived there when he was first married to Rita. He'd gone there to escape all his boozy mates, like Paddy, but it didn't work and Vic was back in the city within a couple of years.

The colour has gone from the sky and it is now dark. But the headlights of this engine are good and Paddy can see well into the distance, which is just as well because it takes a lot of track to stop a train like this. You need a lot of warning. You need to be able to see into the future, and with headlights like these you can. Paddy holds up his old, tea-stained mug to the fireman who takes it and shakes his head. One day, says his fireman, one day you will wash this thing. Never, says Paddy, saying that the tea would lose its flavour. He takes his tea black, with two sugars, and the inside of his mug is encrusted with the years.

The fireman rises from his seat, takes his own mug with him, and steps down into the nose of the engine. Just before his head disappears he grins at Paddy, waving his mug in the air and threatening to clean it for him. You bloody dare, says Paddy to the already disappearing face of the young fireman, and it'll be the last bloody thing you do. His eyes quickly return to the track in front of him, noting that it is the first humorous exchange between them. There might just be a bit of cheek in the young coot yet. A fireman's got to have a bit of cheek, keeps the driver amused. A bit of cheek, but not too much.

In the solitude of the cabin Paddy concentrates on the track. But for a moment he slides the window open beside him. A sudden rush of summer air enters the cabin and he looks up to the shadowy clouds and three-quarter moon, briefly dwelling on the colour of the sky earlier that evening.

There is a goods train approaching the town from the border. It is a small train, only eight carriages, carrying mostly wheat and grain for the Melbourne silos and warehouses. The locomotive hauling it all is an R Class steam engine. Designed in Melbourne and built in Glasgow, it is the last of the large passenger engines, a steam age answer to the oncoming age of the diesel locomotive. A passenger engine, hauling farmer's grain.

The driver is from a border town whose life revolves around the railways. If the station dies, because the engines won't need to take on water there any more, the town dies. He is sixty-four years old and has driven steam all his life. To him the R Class engine, with its sweeping red guards that give it the appearance of movement even when standing still, is a beautiful piece of work. A functional but eminently pleasing combination of uncluttered lines and concentrated power. This engine can go. It can match any of the new diesels, and with a well-made fire in its furnace by a fireman who knows what he's doing, it could roll the lot of them.

This man is not a Big Wheel driver. He has never thought of himself as a great driver or a driver of distinction. He thinks of himself simply as a good, honest driver. A craftsman. He has no pretensions and is normally very cautious. But tonight, to satisfy his mind and affirm his faith in the engine he is driving he has let it go and taken the train to the maximum speed limit allowed, and even beyond. As a consequence this goods train is moving.

It is uncharacteristic driving on his part, but he is a year from retirement and he wants, once and for all, to be satisfied in his own mind that this engine can do everything he thinks it can. And he may cop a fine for speeding for the first time in his driving career. So be it. He has been a model of caution all his life and one blemish in the Safe Working book at administration at Spencer Street will not undo all of that.

Besides, there is no danger. There is only the *Spirit* coming from Melbourne. He has all the time in the world to slow the engine down, ease back on the reglator and be ready to slip into the loop on the other side of the town, let the *Spirit* pass, then slip out the other side and continue on to Melbourne.

He checks his fob watch, then looks ahead along the track, listening to the engine. It's humming, and there's more in reserve. Every second, every click of the rails, confirms his beliefs.

26.

The Red Letter Box

On the other side of the street, shadowy figures in the twilight, the two sons and the daughter of a Ukrainian family are gathered round their new letter box, thoughtfully examining the square, wooden container. It is unpainted. In their best clothes, the three children are quietly discussing the box.

Michael suddenly leaves his parents and runs across the dirt street to join his friends. As he nears them he can hear that they are speaking in Ukrainian and he can tell from the manner of their conversation that it is an important one. When Michael stops at the front gate they do not look up at him at first. They are still and concentrating on the letter box. When the oldest of the three children notices Michael, the others turn to him as well, greeting their friend in English.

Michael's parents have stopped walking and are standing on the opposite side of the street, observing the four children now gathered round the letter box. Rita smiles to herself because with their chins on their hands, and their arms folded, or on their hips, they look like three old men and an old woman. After a moment of silence the eldest looks up to Michael.

'What do you think?'

Michael is puzzled.

'About what?'

Of course, the eldest brother smiles, Michael has only just joined their discussion.

'The letter box,' he says, 'What colour should we paint it?'

Michael nods, now understanding the situation. The group is silent again until the eldest brother speaks up once more.

'Anna,' he says, pointing to his sister, 'wants it to be the same colour as the house.'

Michael looks at their square, weatherboard house and nods in agreement. But the eldest brother shakes his head. 'Gregor,' he adds, pointing to his younger brother, 'wants it to be green.'

Michael turns up his face and this time he shakes his head.

'Well,' says the younger brother, 'You think of something.'

All three then turn to Michael. His parents are calling for him to rejoin them, but his three friends are waiting for him to say something. He knows he has to speak, and quickly.

'Why not red?'

The three stare back at him, momentarily speechless.

'Red?', asks the eldest brother.

'Yes. Why not?'

The three children then turn to each other and begin laughing, clapping their hands, slapping their thighs, and repeating the word 'red'. His simple suggestion has become an immense, one-word joke. And even though he spoke the word it clearly means something else to the others, and he is suddenly outside the circle of their friendship unable to understand the significance of what he has just said.

'Why not? he asks, now annoyed with his friends.

When they see his annoyance they stop laughing and the younger brother speaks.

'It is impossible.'

'Impossible,' the elder brother repeats, followed by the sister. 'The whole street,' the oldest brother continues, 'will think we are communists.'

'Do you want the whole street to think we are communists?' the sister adds.

'But why would they?' Michael asks, confused.

'Because of the letter box,' the oldest says, as if it were obvious.

'Red,' says the younger brother, 'stands for communism.'

'Don't you know that?' the sister says.

'No.'

'Well, it does.'

'Oh,' Michael nods.

'Do you understand now?' the oldest asks.

'Yes,' Michael nods, 'I understand.'

'Good,' his friend nods, 'It is important to know.'

Michael's parents call to him again. Before he goes, to make amends, he suggests another colour.

'Then why don't you paint it white like Anna says? Like the house?'

The senior brother nods thoughtfully, like an old man, in his best tie and shirt.

'White is better, but it's still difficult. In the old country the Whites were opposed to the Reds.'

'Oh,' Michael now nods learnedly.

'Yes,' adds the older brother. 'This is true. Do you believe me?'

'Yes,' says Michael. 'Yes, I do.'

'There were two sides, the Whites and the Reds. But that was in the old country and our parents don't want to remember it. And if we paint the letter box white it will only remind them, and we don't want that. Do you understand?'

Michael nods slowly, half-heartedly, frowning slightly.

'But your house,' he says, pointing to the square, weatherboard structure. 'Your house is white.'

There is a sudden silence, and, horrified, the older brother turns to the house as if seeing it for the first time, and as if a whole new problem has only just occurred to him.

It is at that moment that Michael's parents call to him again, urgently this time, and Michael leaves the three children, the oldest with his chin resting on his hand, the younger brother with his arms folded, and the sister with her hands by her side. All three have re-assumed the attitudes they had before Michael arrived. All three have returned to silence. Only now, they are contemplating the house.

Michael rejoins his parents and his mother asks what they were talking about. Michael explains and his mother shakes her head slightly, then glances back at the three wise children still studying their house. They are nearing George Bedser's now and Vic has drifted on a few paces ahead, leaning forward as he walks, as if leaning into a strong wind.

It is a walk that almost defines a generation in itself, for Vic was born at the end of the first war and grew up during the Depression. His hands as he strides up the street to the Englishman's house are in his pockets, his shoulders are hunched, and his head is lowered. It is a winter walk in summer. Above all, it is a walk that only knows one direction, and that is forward. A walk which assumes that everything left behind is not worth going back to, and everything to the side, anywhere within the range of peripheral vision, is a potential distraction. But it is not a walk that embraces the future. Rather, it is one that reluctantly presses forward, as if there is nothing else to be done, no other way, a walk that always acknowledges in its hunched wariness, the distinct possibility that any one step might mark the return of disaster and misery. One learns to walk like that in difficult times, and once the walk is learnt it is never forgotten.

27.

Love Songs

The final house before George Bedser's does not have a number. It has a name. Eden. It stands for Evie and Dennis. The Doyles. Together they make Eden. It's a kind of joke. The couple has only been in the street for six months.

He is a transport driver. When he is not at home sleeping, he is driving along the highway at night. He drives to all the big cities, sleeps in the truck while it is unloaded, then drives back when it is loaded again. She washes dishes at the golf club. When she is finished, more often than not, she comes back to an empty house.

Evie, is young, twenty-seven. In summer, when she returns from washing dishes, she leaves the front and back doors of the house open, turns the radio on, sits on the front porch, and drinks and smokes till the night is cool enough for sleeping.

Michael's mother is not very good at making friends. Sometimes, she can look like she prefers to keep to herself. And sometimes, like tonight, she wears dresses that she, and everybody else knows, are just a bit too good for this street. So she doesn't make friends much. But if his mother has a friend in the street at all, this woman who sits on the front porch of her square, weatherboard house with the black wrought-iron name 'Eden' screwed to the boards below the front light, listening to the radio while her husband is on the highway, drinking and smoking till it is cool enough to sleep, this woman is her friend.

One night, a few months earlier, the first of the warm nights, Rita had to get out of the house. Vic had been late back from the bar in the golf club and the house was silent because nobody was talking, and suddenly Rita had to get out. She threw her apron onto the floor and slammed the front door as she stepped out onto the dirt road and began walking, not sure where she was going or how far she would walk before the anger left her. Near the bottom of the street she heard a radio and a nameless song and slowed as she passed the house. On the front porch she saw a young woman, drinking beer and smoking. She knew this was the new couple's house, and, as she slowed, she introduced herself.

An hour later, Rita walked back towards the golf course end of the street towards the silent house and back into her kitchen where she picked up the apron again with the faint smell of beer on her breath.

Now, when Vic is away working at night, and when Evie's husband is also away, the two women sit on the front porch together, while Michael sits in the lounge room staring at the new television that is barely watched. Evie has no interest in it. She prefers the songs on the radio, and her husband is rarely home at nights. So, with the lounge-room windows open to catch any breeze that might come along, Michael slumps on the couch with a lemonade and biscuits, and watches whatever appears on the screen.

Evie, whose hair, short and wavy, is always brushed, and who always looks made up as if ready to go out at any minute, drinks cool beer on the porch. Michael's mother either sips soft drink or a mixture of lemonade and beer. And the only time Michael has seen his mother smoke cigarettes is on the front porch of this woman's house while they talk quietly and confidentially the way friends do.

Sometimes, when nothing is being said on the television, Michael can just hear what they are saying through the open lounge-room windows. And usually, Evie speaks of going somewhere. But when his mother asks where, she says she doesn't know. And then she adds that she keeps on forgetting she's alive. Then she tells his mother she should remember that too, and they talk a lot about going places. Together and alone. But they never say exactly what it is they are so intent on leaving. Or if they do it is when they speak low because they know that Michael is just next door in the lounge room, that the windows are open, and that he has ears like a young elephant and a memory to match.

On those nights, when Evie rises from the porch and walks back into the house, into her kitchen to take beer from the refrigerator, she will pause by the lounge-room door and ask Michael if he wants more lemonade or biscuits. And when Michael tells her he doesn't, she informs him that she will close the lounge-room door so that she can turn the radio on without disturbing him.

Michael always shrugs his shoulders and says he doesn't mind, but she quietly closes the door on him all the same. When the music is playing he can still hear the two women talking, but he can no longer distinguish their words. They are talking about staying and going, he knows that. But he won't hear their words any more because the radio is playing.

Now, walking past the house, the wrought-iron name lit up for the street to see, Michael hears the sound of beer glasses tinkling from past nights, he hears the tearing sound of a match being struck. And as he stares at that porch, he hears once again their serious, private words, spoken low.

And even now, as they leave her house and approach the Englishman's front gate, Michael can hear music on the front porch. They are songs about love, about the lovers who leave and those who have been left behind but who stay lovers anyway, because they fall in love with their memories. And, underneath these songs, years from now, he will hear the two women, hear the murmur of their voices, through the songs and the singing, the guitars and the violins. He will always hear their voices, but not their words, and the porch will remain a place of mystery.

At that moment Evie is standing at the sink in the golf course kitchen. The dirty dishes are stacked on the side of the sink and when the kitchen door swings open the waitress adds to the stack. The noise of the dining area comes in with the waitress. Evie turns in time to catch a glimpse of the large room where the club members, their wives, children, grandmothers and grandfathers all sit stuffing schnitzels and steaks into their mouths before drawing on the large mugs of chilled beer on the tables. It's a hot night, everybody's out eating and the dishes will keep coming till the kitchen closes and the members and their families spill out into the car park for the uncertain drive home. In the warm darkness later that night the restless young lovers of the suburb will tumble over and round each other, rolling on the golf course greens or inexpertly grappling with each other's buttons under the ferns that line the tees, leaving the discarded evidence of their Saturday night for the gardeners to clean away on Monday morning.

Evie returns to the dishes. She always has a cigarette on the table behind her. Most of the time it burns down to the filter, but occasionally she pauses and drags on it through rubber gloves while staring out through the kitchen window onto the bins outside. She's twenty-seven. She feels old. A harmless tumble on the green with some young fool seems like a good idea. Evie returns to the dishes. The sooner they're done, the sooner she can go to Bedser's party. She is a kind person with a generous nature. A good friend. But Evie sometimes does rash things. And tonight – with the heat, the endless bloody dishes, and her husband out on the road again – is just the night for a bit of rash behaviour.

Rita glances at the front porch of Evie's house. The front door is closed, the windows are shut up, and, apart from the porch light which illuminates the name, the house itself is in twilight. Beside her, Vic grunts quietly as he contemplates the bloody fool idea of calling anything Eden.

28.

George Bedser

George Bedser's house sits in a small hollow at the end of the street. It is made from plain weatherboard, painted white, and has a small rose garden which is struggling to survive the summer. The front door is open, and inside, the voices of the first guests can be heard. The colour has left the sky now and the white paint of the house has turned to grey and dark shadows. But the lights of all the front rooms are turned on, and the porch light and the party lights across the front hang in the air like fake fruit.

As Vic, Rita and Michael enter the front gate and walk up the newly concreted pathway that leads to the front door of the house, they see George Bedser, in his starched white shirt, waiting for them on the porch.

He is a small man, five feet four, his hair is thinning and grey and he has a cautious smile. He is a shipbuilder from Liverpool, a welder who spent twenty-three years in the shipyards of the city welding giant sheets of iron to the frames of trawlers, tankers, ferries and ocean liners. The famous, the forgotten, the numerous coal boats of the city, it was all the same. He was born in the city, married in the city, and spent all his life there. His family, his brothers and sisters, and all their families are still there. And he would be too. But his wife suddenly left him one day for a spiv. No warning, no tell-tale signs. Suddenly she was gone, with a drifter in a slick suit who sold something or other door to door. He heard things from time to time, but never saw her again. Nor did he want to. What was the point? She wasn't his Vera any more. She was someone else. And George Bedser loved his Vera.

Patsy was just fourteen then, now she is twenty-one. They spent two more years in Liverpool while they were waiting for permission to emigrate. Finally, one drizzling June day the two of them boarded the *Otranto* and left England for good. He had never sailed before but he was unconcerned by the journey. He knew a good ship.

Tonight his daughter is getting engaged, and, in the absence of his family, George Bedser has invited the street. And why not? He and his daughter have lived in the street for five years now, longer than most. He found work easily on the docks when he arrived, but he is a quiet man, one who has always stuck to his family and is unused to making friends, and so he made none at the docks. If he has a sense of family now, of community, it is the community of the street he has come to live in. Even if he never indulges in long conversations with his neighbours, even if he never much hangs about at the local shops passing time, he has still come to regard the street, and the people in it, as his.

As Vic, Rita and Michael step onto Bedser's small front porch, shake his hand and meet the shy, cautious smile in his eyes, they compliment him on the look of the house; on the coloured lights, the ribbons on the door, and the white, yellow and red roses along the front fence. He nods, raises his eyebrows and is about to respond, to make some comment about the dry soil, when his daughter joins them and he is distracted. His eyes become bright, as if bright with wine, even though he has had nothing to drink.

Patsy wears a bright, swaying summer dress; her hair, cut with a fringe and held in place by a velvet band, is auburn; her eyes are green. Her skin has the translucence of a young woman and, immediately,

Rita admires that skin and remembers what it was to be twenty-one. Patsy welcomes the three guests, shakes their hands, winks at Michael, then turns to her father, grinning, and Rita can see there's cheek in that grin. But it's George Bedser that Rita is really watching, for he hasn't taken his eyes off his daughter since she stepped onto the porch.

There he is, George Bedser, his eyes on his daughter, his eyes only for his daughter, and she's looking away. He can't take his eyes off her because he probably never thought he'd be able to get her this far by himself. But he has. I wonder if Vic sees the look in the old man's eyes too, but he's only looking at her. She's talking to me, she's talking to Vic, she's talking to Michael and I wish she'd turn just once and catch the look in her father's eyes.

Patsy is being called from the hallway of the house. She hears her name but does not respond. Patsy is puzzled, not so much by the sound of her name as the voice that is calling to her. She looks out across the yard, to the darkness beyond the suburb, and for that moment the party smile leaves her face. Her eyes are suddenly sad and Michael watches the line of those eyes, calculating the direction she's looking in, somewhere out beyond the mills, beyond the station. But her party eyes return as quickly as they went, she finally responds to the call and a young man steps out onto the porch.

'There you are.'

This is Allan, the young man who is going to marry Patsy. On hearing his voice George Bedser takes his eyes off his daughter and scrutinises the young man with a slight smile in his eyes. Patsy's young man is twenty-one, his hair is a little long and brushed back in the modern style. But he's no lair. Bedser nods quietly to himself. He's a good lad. A local lad. Quiet. Some might even call him gormless. In fact, some of the locals do. But he's just quiet. Besides, that doesn't bother George Bedser. He's seen the flashy types, the loud ones, come and go, at work, at war, and they're usually the first to disappear when they're needed. More than likely, it's the gormless ones who get the job done when the job needs doing. They have their time, quietly meet their moment, without too much fuss, then go back to being the gormless types who sit in corners at parties and dances, content to watch. No, Bedser doesn't mind the young lad at all, though he's never said as much.

It is then that George Bedser gestures to the inside of the house, talking of pies, rolls, biscuits, beer and sparkling wines. As they all step inside a slow song begins on the record player, and in the far part of the lounge room a couple is already dancing.

George Bedser is summoned to the front door again the moment they're inside. And for the next ten minutes the street, family by family, enters George Bedser's house and the party begins.

29.

The View from Pretty Sally

Jimmy's car approaches the top of the hill, the name of which has always amused him. Pretty Sally. He changes gears and the car lurches forward. And as he leaves the thick darkness of the river valley behind him, as he finally reaches the top of the hill, he slows the Austin Wolseley briefly. For there, spread out beneath him, washed up onto the wide coastal plain below, are the foaming lights of the city. And the nearest of those lights, some thirty minutes away, is the suburb to which he is travelling.

He's been selling hi-fi's door to door in the country through the week, now his week is finished and he's driving back to the city. He knows the highway will take him on to Patsy Bedser's suburb. He has been thinking about nothing else all day.

The Wolseley noses over the hill and rolls down the long, winding slope that leads onto the plain. The car is simply rolling like a large ball. Jimmy's foot is on the brake, slowing the car at the curves then easing off the pedal when the road straightens out. It is a long, gradual descent and the car feels for a moment like it is falling out of the sky. There is a cigarette in Jimmy's mouth and from time to time he flicks the ash out the open window without taking his eyes off the road. The radio is loud.

It is a clear night, no cloud, no rain, as there nearly always is on this hill. But it is getting dark and Jimmy occasionally squints into the glare of oncoming headlights. At times he catches his reflection in the suddenly illuminated rear-vision mirror. His hair is long. Brushed back. He takes pride in being a teddy boy. And when a voice quietly insists that he not take the turn-off to Patsy's Bedser's for there is no place for him at the party, he ignores it, singing to the songs that come on the radio, occasionally thumping the dashboard as if it were a drum. On the seat beside him he has a small stack of the latest forty-fives. They come with the job. Jimmy is driving with one hand on the wheel.

The lights from the houses gradually become more numerous, less scattered. Jimmy is on the coastal plain now and the lights of the city are only noticeable for the glow they create in the sky. He is approaching that hazy boundary where the darkness of the country merges with the illuminated city night. Jimmy is tired. He stares at the road in silence as it follows a small creek then turns left up the last of the hills before reaching the edges of the city.

As the Wolseley crosses the railway lines, the red, asphalt pathway that leads up to the station, the rail siding, and the flour mills on his left, Jimmy slows the car and studies the intersection in front of him.

He turns right and as he slowly drives along the old wheat road he notices that the television repairman's shop window, usually aglow with the blue light of his television display, is boarded up with cardboard and wood. He passes the war memorial at the front of the RSL where a large bunch of fresh flowers lies resting at the base of it. There are, he reflects, always fresh flowers at its base. At least, whenever he has passed it.

The black Wolseley glides slowly past the old, double-storey Victorian terraces that house the greengrocer and the butcher. On the opposite side of the street, to his left, is the weatherboard Presbyterian church. At the dirt intersection before him he will turn left, then right at the playing field of the school.

Above him the comet moves slowly across the suburb, while the Wolseley quietly advances, and while Jimmy inspects the tall pines that line the northern border of the school as they sway in the moonlight.

The Wolseley is now parked in the shadows at the corner of the street. The engine has not been long idle and is still warm from the journey. The radio is turned low. Jimmy is sitting in the dark, behind the wheel, smoking and watching the house at the bottom of the street. All its rooms are illuminated and coloured party lights, red, green and yellow, are hanging from the guttering at the front of the house. The porch is lit-up, the windows have been opened, and music from the hi-fi that he sold to Patsy Bedser last autumn is audible, even from the corner of the street where Jimmy sits inside the black Wolseley.

From time to time guests at the party escape the house onto the front lawn. They stand, smoking, talking quietly and hoping to catch some of the cool evening breeze that is drifting in from the schoolyard, through the pines, and over the yards and houses of the street.

Jimmy is looking up the dirt road before him, watching the comings and goings of the party, sure that in the darkness of the street corner he is hidden from view.

Two women are standing near the front gate. One has red hair and is wearing a floral evening dress with a single bold strap across the right shoulder. It is not the type of dress he expects to see in this kind of street. The other woman appears to have longer hair and wears a dark dress that merges with the shadowy light. She looks impatient in her manner with the other woman, but it is difficult to be sure. In another corner of the yard, three men are gathered in a small circle, the tips of their cigarettes aglow. They are staring down at the dried lawn at their feet, nodding occasionally, not saying much.

The remainder of the party is inside the house, talking, listening to the music or dancing to the songs. All of them, the street that has been invited, the father whom he has never met, Patsy Bedser's fiancé, and Patsy Bedser herself. All of them, no more than a minute's walk from where he is. But Jimmy makes no move to approach the house. He stays behind the wheel of the car, observing the guests who come and go as they step from the porch, seeking the cool outside air, before rejoining the festivities.

All the time, the Wolseley sits quietly in the shadows at the corner of the street.

30.

Night

From the kitchen window, looking back in the direction of the golf course, Michael can see out over the vacant paddock next door. Like all the paddocks on the street it is covered with Scotch thistle and long grass. The peach glow has left the sky. The stars are sparkling like the cut-glass bowls in the lounge room. Michael walks toward the open back door of the house and steps out into the yard. To his right the comet, high in the western part of the sky, is slowly passing over the railway lines, over the cutting that leads into the station, having taken the whole summer to get there from the flour mills.

The dark silhouettes of the schoolyard pines loom before him in the next street. He's climbed the tallest of those pines and knows the view from the top. He has charted his suburb in the map of his mind and knows its streets and houses and landmarks. He can see it all clearly even now, as if he were still perched at the top of the tallest of those pines and the suburb were spread out beneath him.

From the yard Michael can see through the back door into the kitchen and the lounge room adjoining it. There is music coming from the record player, and as the house fills, the talk and the laughter becomes louder. Inside, he can see the families from the street, the Millers, the Bruchners, the Youngers, Mr Van Rijn, the Barlows, the Bedsers and all their friends that he's never met and will probably never see again. And if he can't see the faces of his neighbours, he can hear their familiar voices, their familiar bursts of laughter or their expressions of surprise. Just as when he hears a certain phrase, a saying called out or shrieked above the usual volume of conversation, he will know that Mr or Mrs so-and-so has arrived, because of the way they speak. Like the way Mrs Barlow turns to her husband in mid-conversation, with everybody standing and watching, and says don't be stupid Desmond. He can hear and see them all. All of them. The whole street.

The vacant paddocks either side of the house are swaying in the darkness, and a light breeze passes through its well-lit windows and open doors. The mills have melted into the night, darkness has descended over the schoolyard cricket pitch where one day Michael will bowl the perfect ball, the factory is silent, the factory owner's Bentley is parked at the end of his long gravel driveway, Skinner's cows have bedded down. In the distance is the faint rattle of the Saturday night city train.

Part Two

Saturday Night

31.

Bedser's Front Yard

The music of the party is behind him. Michael is facing the front fence of the Bedsers' house, at the edge of a circle of light created by the streetlight, throwing a worn tennis ball against the pickets. He throws the ball, the ball rebounds and he catches it without letting it touch the ground. His goal is to reach twenty without dropping a catch. But it is difficult. Sometimes the ball hits the picket at an awkward angle and Michael has to dive onto the lawn to take the catch like they do on the television when the cricket is played. Lindwall, Harvey, O'Neill. They all practise their catching like this and so does Michael.

It is a game that absorbs Michael for hours when he is not bowling against his back fence. Especially the hours between the end of school and the beginning of evening when he is waiting for his parents to return from work. In this way hours pass, the day ends, and the evening is upon him before he knows it.

At the moment he is counting his catches. Seventeen. He is so concentrated on completing the task he has set himself that he no longer hears the music from the party behind him. He no longer hears the laughter, the voices, raised in argument or exclamation. All he sees is the shadowy line of pickets before him, all he hears is the sound of the ball as it rebounds from the fence, then a small slap in the night, as the worn tennis ball hits the back of his hands.

But something distracts him. A car has just entered the street. It has not entered the street at any speed, recklessly disturbing the dirt of the road, creating a spectacle and drawing attention to itself. No, this is not why he has noticed it and why he is suddenly distracted. He has noticed the car from the corner of his eye because it has slipped into the street quietly, almost silently. Like it doesn't want to be noticed. And, for that reason, Michael has noticed it.

He straightens up, the ball still now in his hand, and examines the dark car parked at the corner of the street. It could be anybody's car. A guest come late to the party. But the car just sits there. The doors don't open. Whoever is in this car doesn't want to be seen. Michael jumps back quickly from the circle of the streetlight and crosses the small front path to the other side of the yard. There, crouched behind a shrub, he can observe the car freely. It is black. He can see the chrome plate shining in the night, outlining the headlamps, the bumper bar and the grille. As his eyes adjust to the light, he focuses more clearly on the car and begins to distinguish its features. It is an Austin Wolseley. Michael knows his cars and this is an English car. With a shock he realises that he knows this particular car from his fishing trips to the country. He knows who is inside it.

When he realises this he slumps back against the corner of the fence and stares blankly back towards the house. He peers quickly over Bedser's white picket fence and he sees a match flare inside the car. The man with the long legs and the black pointed boots is there. Watching the party. Absent-mindedly Michael tosses the tennis ball from hand to hand, creating faint slaps in the night.

The front door of the house opens and his mother and her friend, the one she drinks beer with on hot nights, step into the yard and walk towards the front gate. They are talking quietly, and Michael can't hear what they are saying. He is conscious once again of the music, and the noise of laughter and talk coming from the party. The door opens again and three men, Mr Bruchner, Mr Younger and a man Michael doesn't know, walk to the other side of the lawn where they stand in a small circle and drink beer and smoke.

Nobody knows Michael is crouched in the corner of the yard. Nobody has noticed the car parked at the corner of the street. Michael has stopped tossing the ball from palm to palm. He is waiting for everybody to go and leave the yard to him once more.

'I just want to be able to look back and say, yea, I had some fun. I lived a bit. That's not much to ask.'

Rita is leaning back against the front gate staring out across the vacant lot next to the Englishman's house. Her friend is nodding, watching the froth die in her beer glass.

'Well, is it?'

Rita's face swings back from the paddock to Evie. There is fire in Rita's eyes and fire in her hair. She pulls the back of her hair out into the evening, tight, as if the strands were strings and she were about to play upon them. Then she lets her hair go and it falls back bobbing about her neck.

'Well?'

'No,' her friend looks up, 'It's not.'

'That's what it comes down to, having fun. I'm thirty-three and I feel like I've had mine. We don't go out any more, we just stay in and stare at the walls. That's not living. But it wasn't always like that. Now everything's just a bloody great effort. What happens?'

'You tell me, I'm married to a truck.'

Rita barely hears. She is distracted, staring out across the paddock again.

'He was so handsome.'

'Still is.'

'You're always calling him handsome. Aren't you?'

Evie doesn't answer. She studies Rita, who is staring out across the swaying vacant lot as if it were a wide, expansive sea leading somewhere else.

'What will you do?'

Rita doesn't look back.

'Give it one last go. But if it doesn't work, I swear, I'm not staying out here for anyone.'

Rita looks around the suburb and shakes her head. For the first time she notices Bruchner, Younger and someone else she doesn't know standing in the front yard near the lounge-room window. The two groups remain closed and do not acknowledge each other. She doesn't like them and they don't like her. Rita knows that. They think she's a snob, but she doesn't care. So be it. Her eyes hover for the moment on the compact bulk of Bruchner, then return to her friend.

'I never thought it would come to this. I thought we'd go on forever. And even when things got difficult, I never thought it could actually end.'

Rita has stopped talking. She is looking out to that vast, private sea again. She can hear the waves now, slapping against each other in the night, smell the open, salty air, hear the call of sea birds. The vacant paddocks of the suburb sway like an ocean leading somewhere.

In time, when the boy is grown and she and Vic have finally gone their separate ways, Rita will cross that ocean and she will see the greater world she yearns for. Even though it seems impossibly far away at the moment, she will go to it, that great, wondrous world that lies beyond the suburb, and the poky houses and the prying eyes. And all those small minds that look you up and down if you try to look a little smart, that take it personally like an insult and brand you a snob if you look a bit stylish. She will travel outside the invisible walls of the suburb and beyond. But she will travel alone. Vic will not be there. He will move north. He will travel on vast desert trains a mile long and drink black tea two miles below the earth's surface in the nickel mines of the inland deserts, but Vic will never travel beyond his own country and Rita will never really understand why. Never really understand that he would be lost, a man out of his element. And so Rita will cross that ocean, but there will always be a part of her that will be looking back, wishing she didn't have to travel it alone. Perhaps, even now, she knows this.

'I'll get Vic. See if I can drag him away from the fridge.'

Evie breaks into her thoughts and she turns back from surveying the dark, open paddocks and looks at Evie as if having returned from a journey and wondering where on earth she is.

'Leave him there.'

'I'll use my charm.'

But Rita is suddenly annoyed.

'Evie, just leave him there.'

'Why?'

'I don't want him dragged here or anywhere.'

'He won't be. Trust me.'

Evie touches Rita's shoulder lightly and leaves her standing by the gate. As she walks back into the party along the narrow, front path, she is already looking through the open windows for Vic, somewhere in there amongst the laughter and the talk. At the front door she hears the flyscreen door shut behind her. On the record player, one song ends, another begins.

Evie moves through the guests, nodding, chatting briefly and moving on, the gathering seeming to part around her as she walks from room to room. She can still smell the detergent on her hands and feel the hot water from all the dishes she washed tonight at the golf course. She's glad there's a party tonight. Her husband has been on the road now a month. The house is almost continually empty and she couldn't face walking back to it alone again as she has for the last four Saturdays. During the week she can face an empty house, but not on Saturdays. Houses shouldn't be empty on Saturdays. Evie likes people around her. She likes a beer and she likes a laugh. And as she walks through the party, she is pleased with the proximity of all these people, as if something could happen. And after a month of lonely Saturdays, on top of all the others, she wouldn't mind that. She savours the closeness of everybody, the laughter, the talk, the music and the dancing.

Outside, Rita is still standing at the front gate staring out across the vacant paddocks, sipping a lemonade and beer. After an hour inside the house she wanted some fresh air. So she's outside. Vic wanted to stay in. She can tell already that he's throwing down the beers faster than he should, but what's the point of saying anything? It won't change a thing, he'll just go on throwing them down. Even faster.

And so she stares out across the wide, swaying sea of vacant paddocks and tries to imagine what another life might be like.

32.

Vic and Evie

I like a woman with a beer in her hand. And there she is. She's walking through the party like she's looking for someone. Her head turning this way and that. She's smiling and nodding. Courteous and polite. But she doesn't really care about any of them. She's looking for someone in particular.

But what she doesn't see is that they're all looking at her. When she's passed their eyes all follow her, looking her up and down. The men and the women. The husbands and the wives. They're looking at her because she's, what shall we say? a mature woman, she's on her own, and she's got a beer in her hand. To some of the women that's a sign of danger. And the way she's walking about, looking for someone or something, as if she's not sure what, and as if she doesn't care anyway, well, that doesn't help. To the blokes on this street she's a bit of a curiosity. They'd like to stop her and talk to her. They'd like a bit of her. But they haven't got what it takes to stop a woman like that. None of them. Not in this street. She's not interested in them and they know it. Not that it's obvious or she lets it show. She's no snob. She's not standoffish. But she scares them a bit. Not that she's the world's best looker. She looks good, all right. And she's a well-built woman. But that's not what she's got. There's a bit of a challenge in the way she's walking about. And this place can see it. The blokes, the women, the husbands and wives who notice her as she passes by. They can all see it. And that's why she scares them. That's why they all stand back a bit. This is the kind of woman who shakes things up.

And there's the way she holds that beer glass. She holds it like a woman who knows her beer. Some women hold a beer glass like a non-smoker holds a cigarette, like they're holding it for someone else. But the way this woman holds her beer glass leaves you in no doubt whatsoever that the beer is hers. Just as she leaves you in no doubt that she knows a few things about beer itself. And a bit more besides.

She's standing in the middle of the room now, like she's lost her way. She's drinking her beer and looking about like she's ready to turn around and go back to wherever she's come from because she can't find who she's looking for. Then she props, she smiles and she waves – at me.

Before I know it she's standing in front of me with an empty beer glass in her hand. That's the other thing I notice, she doesn't sip the stuff, she drinks it.

'Hello handsome.'

That makes me laugh. Like she's stepped out of a movie or something. Maybe she thinks she has. She's always calling me handsome. I like it, but it makes me laugh.

We're standing near the back door, there's a bit of a breeze coming in through the wire, and she's holding her beer out. I fill the glass with a bottle I've stashed away.

'I've just left Rita,' she says. 'She's at the front gate. You should go talk to her.'

'Oh.'

I'm nodding. Should I? It's not my fault she's out there and I'm in here. Is it? Naturally, I don't say this, but I catch her eye as I'm thinking it and it's as good as said.

'I promised her I'd get you out there.'

'Did you?'

'I like to keep my promises. So I might just hang around till you do.'

Suit yourself, I'm thinking. Suit yourself. But personally, I can't see the point in coming to a party if you're going to stand around in the yard all night. Well, that's what I'm thinking. I'm not sure what she's thinking but I give her the once over and with a bit of a shock I see there's a look there. It's just a trace, but it's there. A look that reminds me of the days before I got hitched. And the music, the grog, the noise and all the people. It all helps. Neither of us is saying anything by now. But it doesn't matter. This is better than talking any day. So we just stand there, side by side, listening to the old songs.

Sometimes it happens like that. You're standing around doing the usual things and in walks a different life. No, not a different one. Not really. But a glimpse of one. It shakes you up a bit.

Like you're driving along this single track in the night. The moon's shining down on the rails and that track looks like it could just stretch out in front of you forever. And you feel like you could just put your feet up, boil the tea, lean back in your seat, close your eyes, and let the bloody thing drive itself. And then you realise that you, you are the bloody thing. It's not driving. You are.

You pass a familiar station. A familiar stop. And then suddenly you spot a side track you've never really noticed before. It might only run for a mile into a wheat silo. It might run for a hundred. Suddenly it looks good. You could go off the rails. No section clearance, no staff in your hand, no permission. Bugger the lot, you might say. And before you know it you're off. And you could be gone and back in a flash. No harm done. Nobody to know anyway. Or you could just take that track and never come back at all.

I see you in another time, sugar. I can see you in another room. With another me. And I hear your talk the way it might sound there. And it sounds good. And suddenly, another time, another place, don't seem so far away.

33.

The End of the Double Bed

Rita is still standing by the front gate staring out across the paddocks that are slowly swaying in moonlight and shadow. The three men standing on the dry lawn near the house are slowly becoming muttering drunks. She doesn't speak to them, they don't speak to her. Past the houses, the low grassy paddocks go on forever. If only there were some trees. Something to break the flat lines of the paddocks, the dirt streets and the square houses that sit on them. But there aren't. The trees have all been swept away to make room for the square houses.

The music of the party is not inviting. She'd like to dance. In her new dress, she'd like to be dancing. The way she used to. The way they used to. There are times when she thinks she was never so happy as when she was dancing. But Vic has started drinking and already she can tell there'll be no dancing tonight.

He can dance, all right. He's one of the best. When he wants to be. Not that he ever dances with me any more. The only dancing he ever does at home these days is when he comes to bed drunk and he's trying to get his trousers off. He does this little jig, hopping from one foot to the other. Sometimes he does a low whistle to accompany himself, and it could even be funny, but it's not. It happens too often, this little jig of his. Then, when he stops hopping from foot to foot, and he finally gets his trousers off, he flops into bed on his back and snores all night. He starts off low, but then he gets into his rhythm. Pretty soon the snores rattle the venetians and the room stinks of grog. Like the stink of a public bar. Not that I've been in one for years, not since I was a child and my mother dragged me through some pub in Prahran one afternoon looking for my papa. But sometimes I'm passing a pub in the city, the door flies open and the stink pours out like bad breath from a drunk's mouth. And that's the smell that fills the bedroom in minutes. Along with the snores. He's on his back with his nose in the air. And sometimes, sometimes the snores come out of him like steam from a train's stack. He's getting a real hooter on him these days. And it's getting bigger and fleshier with the years and the booze. Pretty soon we'll be able to stand him in the hallway and use him as a hat stand, 'cause he's getting the kind of hooter you could hang your hat on. And just when he's sleeping quietly he snorts, wakes himself for a few minutes and mumbles something in the dark. Then he bounces around on the bed like there's nobody else in it, before he's snoring again and filling the room with all the grog he's just filled himself up with. So there's no more dancing in our house. Just a drunken jig as he takes his pants off before bed and a night of snoring.

That was the end of the double bed. Even as I said it to him one morning, after he'd snored his way through the night and I'd lain there beside him trying to sleep in between the snores. Even as I said it, even as I opened my mouth and my speech crossed the kitchen table towards him, I could hear my mama's words in my ears saying once the double bed is gone the marriage is gone.

But I didn't care, and that old, dark, stained, barge of a bed, that took up half the room anyway, was taken apart and carried out the front door in bits. I hated it anyway. It reeked of old rooms. Old people. Old bones, old skin and old breath. I'd watched my mother slowly dying in a bed like that,

...w I felt like I was doing the same thing.
...me way. We bought it second hand and
e... we bought it the thought occurred to me
that ... e died in beds like that. And some nights,
I swear, I could still see the ghosts of all the old
things who'd ever slept and died in that bed, sitting
up in it, white-faced and white-haired with their
potties in their hands and their doyleys over their
potties, just like mama. No, I was glad to see the
ugly thing go. It gave me the creeps.

So the old bed went out in bits, and in came two
single beds of clear, varnished pine. As soon as they
were assembled they lit the room up. I picked them
because I knew they would. And I could see them
with clean sheets and blankets, and the bright new
quilts I'd bought the week before.

I had my own bed again. My own bedside lamp.
My own corner of the room.

Rita's eyes leave the vacant paddocks and turn back
to the party. She can see the silhouettes of the guests
through the windows of the house as they dance and
move about from room to room. There's an old song
playing and she can hear Bedser's English friends
singing along the way the English do when they all
get together and an old song is played.

This makes her smile, and as she's smiling Evie
opens the screen door and steps back on to the

front path. She has a brown bottle of chilled beer in her hand and smiles at Rita as she walks towards the front gate.

'No luck', she says. 'I'll try him again when we've drunk this. I know where he is and he doesn't look like he's moving.'

Evie tilts the bottle and pours the chilled beer into Rita's glass. And as Rita listens to the sing-along inside, and as she watches the dancing bubbles in her glass rise to the surface, she's glad of the company. And the beer tastes good. She might even have another. Not that she can keep up with Evie, because Evie is throwing them back a bit.

34.

Vic's Women

'Bye handsome,' she says, still holding that beer glass and making her way through the party and back out to the front yard.

She's an impressive woman. And she knows she is too. A woman who grows on you. The more you see of her, the more impressive she is. You don't see women like that now. Not often. At least I don't. Not with that kind of look. They went out with the war. All except her. She's the last of a kind.

I used to know women like that. I don't any more, but I did. I used to get them around the backs of the dances. And in the back lanes. Anywhere quiet and private. I'd pull their pants down. Their slippery nylon pants. Their frilly pants. Their lily-white pants. In the back streets, up against a fence. Anywhere quiet. I'd pull their pants down and empty out the old sago bag right there.

Afterwards, we'd go back to the dance hall and we'd dance some more, or listen to the band, or lose each other in the crowd. Those were the days. Now, as soon as I hear someone say to me it'll be just like the good old days I know it'll be bulldust. It's one of those lines that gives the game away straight off. The fact is we don't have days like that any more. And we don't have women like that any more. Except for her. 'Bye handsome,' she says, with that look in her eye. And she knows exactly what she's doing. And I thought her type went out with the war. Get a woman like that and it just might be like the old days. It just might.

But what have I got now? Huh? A single bed. A bloody single bed. I've got mine, and madam's got hers. Two bloody single beds.

Vic is leaning against a wall, away from the party, near the back door. Evie has just left the lounge room. She quickly disappears, leaving the dancing and all the talk behind her while she returns to the front yard of the house to rejoin Rita.

Vic is now leaning against a wall by himself. He is filling a large pot glass with beer and watching the foam settle before taking a large gulp. He has reached that point in his drinking when his humour begins to fade, when the smiles begin turning into sneers. When his eyes lose their affability and harden. When nothing is right, and there's everything to gripe about. When he'd prefer to be by himself. When he'd prefer to be what he was. Precisely that point in the evening where he should stop drinking. But he doesn't. Instead, he watches the foam settle in his glass, then takes a giant swig.

Outside, on the front lawn, the two women are silent. There is a song playing on the record player. A slow song. A familiar ballad that is already old enough to be layered with memory. Evie is swaying slightly to this song, swaying her hips from side to side, as if she were dancing with an invisible partner.

Rita is looking down at her feet oblivious of the music, of her friend and of the party until she is suddenly drawn back into the world by the sound of a worn tennis ball hitting the wooden pickets of Bedser's front fence.

35.

The Slap

The ball rebounds and Michael pockets it. He has been in the front yard for an hour now and that black car hasn't shifted, nor has the driver left it. Michael eyes it, perched at the corner of the street, as he walks along the path to the front door. The shadow of a driver is barely visible behind the windscreen.

Inside he passes the quiet figure of Mr Van Rijn who is looking lost without his wife. He nods and Mr Van Rijn returns the greeting without smiling. Perfume and cigarette smoke hang in the still air of the lounge room. Men, their faces shining with fresh haircuts and close shaves are smiling and laughing under the light. The women, in summer dresses, with strings of imitation pearls and coloured stones about their necks, are seated along a row of chairs along the far wall or standing near the windowsills to catch a breeze.

As Michael approaches a large drinks table and pours himself a glass of lemonade he spots his father talking to their next-door neighbour, Mr Barlow, beside the refrigerator. With one look he knows that his father has already drunk too much. He knows the slouch, the lost look beginning to appear in his eyes, the mechanical jangling of loose change in his trouser pocket, the grip of the beer glass. He knows it all. And every now and then he hears his father's booming laugh carrying across the kitchen to the lounge room. His father may be laughing, but he knows his father's laughter can disappear as soon as it erupts.

Someone beside him suddenly slaps their arm and holds up the remains of a mosquito for the examination of those around him. The man then drops the dead insect into an ashtray and the conversation behind Michael resumes. But Michael still hears that slap on the arm.

There was a sound like steaks being slapped down on a bare laminex table. When steaks are thrown onto a laminex table, with force, the impact produces both a slap and a thud. Two sounds, but simultaneous.

He remembers a hot night, like tonight. Possibly, even, a Saturday night. Michael was small. Much smaller than he is now. He had walked from the kitchen into the hallway that leads up to his parents' room. It was dinner time but the empty plates were still sitting on the kitchen table.

His father had returned late again that evening with the dirt of the street all over him. He had walked into the kitchen with a cheery hello as if nothing were wrong, as if he hadn't brought the smell of the public bar with him, and as if he weren't covered in the dust and dirt of the street. When he disappeared into the bedroom Michael's mother had followed him, and that was when it started.

It all happened quickly. One moment he was seated in the kitchen waiting for his dinner, the next he was drawn into the hallway by this sound, like raw steak being slapped onto a table.

The door to his parents' room was shut but he could hear their voices and as he neared the door they become louder. He heard his mother's voice, then his father's. And standing at the door he could even hear the words they were using.

'You'll drag us all down to the gutter with you. You were in the gutter when I first met you – and I wish to God I never had – and you're still there. Look at you.'

His father's voice was weary. Almost bored.

'You're a nun. It's like living in a convent. No wonder you haven't got any friends.'

'Look at yourself. You've got the gutter all over you. That's where you belong. In the filth. If you love it so much go back to it. But you're not taking us there. You're all gutter, aren't you? From head to foot. Wherever you go you bring the gutter with you. You bring the gutter into our house. It's never far away, the gutter. Any gutter.'

It was then that his father had snapped and his voice became loud. He was telling his mother to stop it. To shut up. But his mother just kept going on about the gutter. And dirt. And filth. Then she was crying. And his father was saying, shut up, shut up, shut up. But his mother kept crying. And although Michael knew he shouldn't open the door, he did.

His mother was sitting on the side of the bed. His father was standing in front of her. His mother was still crying and his father was still telling her to stop it. But the more he told her to stop it, the more she cried. Then, with great force, his father's hands came together. He was standing in front of his mother telling her to stop it, when one palm suddenly hit the other palm. And the sound it made was like steaks being slapped down on a bare laminex table.

It was then that his mother looked up and noticed Michael standing at the door. At first she quickly turned away, as if she didn't want Michael to see her face. But he had, and just as quickly she turned back to him, waving her hand in the air, and telling Michael to go away. His father's hands were still together, glued at the point of impact, the sound was still in the air, and his father's eyes were blank as he stared at Michael in surprise. His mother waved Michael away again, and he quietly closed the door as he left.

He didn't turn the light in his room on. Instead he let his footsteps be guided by the moonlight entering the window through the open curtains at the side of the house. Slowly, he pulled the eiderdown back, and, after removing his slippers, climbed onto the bed.

In the wonderful, quiet darkness of his room, he lay down, pulled the eiderdown over his head, closed his eyes, and imagined that he was sleeping.

Michael eyes the dead insect lying amongst the butts of the ashtray in front of him. He hears his father's laughter again, listens briefly to the conversation behind him and notes the English accents of Mr Bedser's friends or the people he works with. Bubbles rise to the top of his glass as he fills it again with the lemonade. When the bubbles have gone he drinks it all at once then turns and walks back out into the front yard. The party sounds fade as the flyscreen door slaps against the house in the night and Michael stands before the front fence once more and takes the worn tennis ball from his pocket, while quickly glancing at the dark car parked at the corner of the street.

36.

A Solitary Game

Mr Bruchner is drunk. He is demonstrating and Michael turns from the front fence in time to see Mr Bruchner's demonstration. His voice is loud and he is speaking to Mr Younger as one would to a child or a trained animal. His hand is raised high above his head and he brings it forward rapidly, hitting an imaginary wall again and again as if he were holding a hammer.

'You see?'

The thin figure of Mr Younger nods and watches once more as the imaginary hammer hits the invisible wall. Their crisp, white shirts, rolled back up past their elbows, are already beginning to crumple. Bruchner drops a cigarette onto the lawn and flattens it with his foot. His mass of matinee curls is falling over his forehead and his eyes are beginning to take on the lost look that drunks have.

'You see?'

Mr Younger sips his lemon squash and nods once more, but Bruchner is not convinced and he begins the demonstration all over again.

When he is finished Bruchner slowly turns from the imaginary wall and tells Mr Younger that his house is no good. That it's a hut. A hovel. A humpy. Ready to fall down. He is telling him that if he had any sense he'd kick the lot over and hire someone who knows what they're doing because he, Mr Younger, is just a bloody storeman who shuffles cardboard boxes around all day and doesn't even know how to hammer a nail in properly. Bruchner, with one of those drunk's smiles that is a twin to a sneer, is enjoying himself. He is telling Mr Younger that his house, if you can call it that, is a disgrace to the street. Or the biggest joke in the street, depending on what type of character you were. Personally, he, Bruchner, can't see the joke, but plenty of others can. The whole street is either laughing or shaking its head. But not Bruchner. He is a tradesman. A plasterer. A perfectionist. And the scrap heap Younger calls his house is an insult. Something that he takes personally. And every night when he drives home from work he's got to look at it because Younger's house is opposite his.

Bruchner then returns to driving his imaginary nail into the night, with increasing force, in the hope that Younger might learn something about the simple art of driving a nail in properly. All the while Mr Younger watches, nodding patiently, his lemon squash in his hand.

Michael watches too, suddenly transfixed by the spectacle of an imaginary hammer being brought forward again and again into imaginary impact with an invisible wall. He watches, again and again, his eyes on the hammer, until, eventually, he can hear the sound it would make.

When he is finished Bruchner offers Mr Younger a cigarette, but Mr Younger doesn't smoke. Bruchner has forgotten that. Or never bothered remembering. Besides, he was only offering the cigarette because Younger was there. Not because he cares. But now that Younger has refused the cigarette, Bruchner has taken it personally. The same way that he takes the offence of Younger's house personally. Younger's offences are mounting and it is then that Bruchner points to the half-empty pot of squash in Younger's hand and says what's that?

He repeats the question, with obvious distaste and tells Mr Younger about his house all over again. Variations on the theme of Younger's house swirl around inside Bruchner with the beer, then spill from his mouth. And when it is said again, when his wide, heavy lips mouth the words that have been swirling round inside him all night, the comments are accompanied by the first of his sneers, the smile falls from his face, and Bruchner, the drunk, has arrived.

When he is finally finished Bruchner stares silently down into Younger's pot of lemon squash, his eyes glazed in struggling thought.

Inside, the butts are mounting in Joy Bruchner's ashtray. From the very beginning of the evening it was recognised by everybody as Joy Bruchner's ashtray. It is understood that she will need that ashtray, and nobody has attempted to use it. A fact that has not gone unnoticed by Joy Bruchner herself, who eyes the mounting pile of butts.

When they first arrived Bruchner sat her in a chair by the window and gave her a beer to sip on. But he has long since gone, and Joy Bruchner hasn't moved from her seat all night. Through the lounge-room window she can see and hear her husband as he is speaking to Albert Younger. As she reaches for her cigarettes, she notes that his voice is rising, knows that it will continue to rise as the evening progresses, and that she will spend a long evening sitting by the window.

* * *

The ball fires back into Michael's hands as he counts the catches. Fifteen. Sixteen. The number quickly mounts. The sounds of the party are all around him, but all he can hear is the slap of the worn tennis ball as it hits the palms of his hands. The moonlight is still strong and he can see the ghostly framework of the house next to old man Malek. But his attention shifts to the black Wolseley at the corner of the street. It's been there for an hour, not moving. Just watching. Nineteen. Twenty.

Something is going to happen. He knows this. A car doesn't stand in the street all night, while its driver sits in shadow watching a party, without something happening. Twenty-one. The front door of Bedser's house opens, revealing the crowded entrance hall. Michael drops the ball. Patsy Bedser sits on the front steps with a drink in her hand and the broad-shouldered bulk of Hacker Paine, the war hero, the veteran of the Kokoda Trail, sits beside her. They are speaking softly, almost confidentially, and their heads incline toward each other like friends in a schoolyard. He can't hear their words above the surrounding talk and the music, but he knows it is a serious conversation and he doesn't want to disturb them. Michael looks from the car to Mr Paine, to Patsy Bedser, and back again. He is on the verge of approaching Mr Paine about the black car on the corner, but something stops him.

Paine is now looking away, no longer talking to Patsy Bedser. No longer talking to anybody. His face has suddenly gone hard. Michael knows he should act. That if he doesn't act soon something will happen.

Bruchner's voice is rising, his speech is slurring, his arms are waving and beer from his glass has just fallen over Younger's new shoes. The tennis ball slaps back into his hands and he loses himself in the game. Twenty-five. Thirty. Forty. Fifty. When the ball finally drops onto the lawn Michael turns to the front steps of the house in time to see Patsy Bedser rise and step back into the entrance hall. Hacker Paine has gone. He hears Hacker Paine's wife asking Patsy Bedser if she's seen her husband, but Patsy didn't see him go. Perhaps he's just inside, she says. But Hacker Paine is nowhere in sight, and suddenly there is no one to tell about the black car on the corner. Beside him Bruchner is relentless, and Mr Younger, his glass of lemon squash gone, is looking like someone who is about to leave but every time he tries Bruchner raises his voice and he stays. Michael's mother and her friend, Evie, are talking next to the front gate. Talk and laughter issue from the opened doors and windows of the house. Everything is louder.

But when the music on the record player suddenly ceases, everybody stops talking. The singing of a small group by the record player, suddenly left unaccompanied and stranded, slowly dies. Laughter from another room subsides. The engagement party holds its breath. There is a moment of silence in which everybody, inside and outside the house, turns in the general direction of the lounge room where the record player is kept.

Then the voice of Patsy Bedser is heard, echoing through the opened rooms of the house to everybody inside, issuing through its opened windows to everybody outside.

She is calling the party to the lounge room. To squeeze in, to squash themselves into the lounge room. And while she hopes the walls of the lounge won't burst she'd like to see everybody in the lounge soon, because her father will make a speech.

37.

The Speeches

Rita edges into the crowded lounge room and finds a spot near an open window beside Joy Bruchner. She is nervous, and she doesn't know why. It's not her giving the speech, but she's nervous all the same. And as she watches George Bedser, shuffling from one foot to the other in front of the gathering and occasionally clearing his throat, she realises she is nervous for him.

The speech isn't her responsibility, but some part of her has assumed responsibility. If it falls flat, if it is a disaster, if George Bedser is left looking like a fool and the party falls to pieces it will be because she didn't will him on. She knows it is ridiculous, but for a moment, Rita is convinced she holds the fate of the party in her hands and she concentrates hard as Bedser begins.

From the moment he starts speaking she knows she can relax. George Bedser is a natural. A reluctant one, but a natural nonetheless. She's never heard him talk so much. But he's standing up there in front of all these people and he's doing it well. And he's got no notes, or paper. He doesn't look like he's prepared anything, but he has. Rita would put money on that. He's been working towards this night for years. And he's proud in that quiet way of his. He's proud of himself for having done it all on his own. He's been thinking about this speech for months, Rita would put money on that too. And it's funny, this speech of George's. Rita didn't think he had a joke in him, but he's got a few all right. And they're all good. She can hear Vic's laugh come from where the fridge is. He's laughing. But at this stage of the game she knows it doesn't mean much. Vic will laugh at anything after a few too many, except himself. But everybody else is laughing too. Including Rita. And nobody's interrupting with any of the usual stupid remarks. They're just letting George get on with it. And so he is. When the applause comes it nearly brings down the house, 'cause everybody knows what it all means to him. And even now, as he's slipping away from the table, he's got that sleepy-eyed smile on his face. And he's pleased with himself, because he knows his job's done now and he can sit back for a bit.

Relieved, Rita leans back against the wall and eyes Patsy's fiancé as he stands to take his place at the front of the room. But her attention strays and soon she is studying Patsy herself because something troubles her about Patsy. With her hair like that, and her dress, and her smile, she looks the part. She laughs and talks like a woman who's happy. Like a woman whose night it is. Whose night has arrived. But Rita feels sad for her and can't figure out why. Maybe she's just sad for herself, but something's not there in Patsy's eyes.

This young man, whose name she doesn't know, is talking to the party. He clearly doesn't want to be talking to anybody, let alone a roomful of strangers. Everybody is listening to him and watching him as he does. They're all summing him up, and he knows it. That's what happens when you talk to a roomful of strangers. They sum you up. But Rita is neither watching him nor listening to him. She's watching Patsy, the way she observes her fiancé, the way she listens then looks down at the floor like she'd give anything to be somewhere else, the way she folds her fingers in and out of each other. Rita is watching all this, and something's not there.

Next to Rita, Joy Bruchner is sitting beside a small mountain of ash. The two women glance at each other, and the most minute of greetings (a nod and a raised eyebrow), passes between them. Joy Bruchner stares at the floor and her eyes have the vacant look of a woman who is resigned to being left alone. The way she has of staring at the floor, or out through the lounge-room window, Rita thinks, is a way of turning herself invisible. For if Joy Bruchner is not looking at the room, then the room is not looking at Joy Bruchner, and nobody will notice her shame. The shame of being the wife who is led to her place, who is given her shandy, her ashtray and her chair, and who is then publicly ignored for the rest of the night. She could simply rise and leave, but that would draw the silent, sympathetic attention of the room, and everybody would then see her sadness and her sadness would be confirmed in the eyes of the street. And so she stares at the floor, or out the window, and her sadness remains inside her where nobody can see it because nobody is looking.

When the room laughs she looks up and her lips form a brief smile. When the room applauds, her hands clap soundlessly along before folding up under her chin. She could easily ignore the laughter and the applause, but when she joins in the laughter, when she brings her hands together in feeble applause, there is a moment when she could almost convince herself that she is one of them, however briefly. One of the room. Like all of those around her. A woman who laughs and listens and applauds and rejoices in the happiness of others. It is her link with them, for without that brittle smile, without the absent-minded slapping together of her palms that she offers as applause, she may as well give up entirely. A ghost by the window who need really not exist at all.

Rita almost reaches out, almost touches the tip of Joy Bruchner's shoulder. For that slapping together of her palms that she offers to the room as applause, even if she doesn't know what she is applauding, that flicker of a smile she offers instead of laughter, the extraordinarily concentrated effort required to produce those two unselfish acts, means that something in Joy Bruchner hasn't entirely given up yet. Rita sees this and that is why she almost touches the tip of Joy Bruchner's shoulder with her right hand.

But she notices Vic. He is beside the fridge and she is about to join him but the young man to whom Patsy Bedser has become engaged is still speaking and Rita leans back against the window, as Joy Bruchner settles back into her chair, her eyes upon the floor, waiting for that moment when the room will either laugh or clap, for that moment when she will bring her hands together in applause, when she will join them all and be one with the room.

38

Mother's Girl

Listen, this voice is saying. He's moved the cutlery on the table in front of him from one side to the other. He's picked up a glass of something sparkling and put it down again. And all the time he's talking, but only part of me is hearing. Listen, the other part says. Listen, that's the voice you'll hear for the rest of your life. That's the face you'll see. A voice dragged into speech, a body dragged to the table. A good face, good hands, a good heart. And look at my dad, looking out from under his eyelids with a satisfied smile on his lips like his life's work is finally over and now he can take a break.

He's watching Allan speaking. And I can tell he likes him with the liking people have for their own kind. And it strikes me that marrying Allan is a bit like marrying your dad. And I like my dad and all, but I don't want to marry him. Maybe that's what my mum thought. Maybe that's what she thought all those years ago, maybe that's what she always knew. That she liked my dad and all, but she didn't really want to marry him. Only she did. And then she had to go through the whole business of getting unmarried. Which would have been difficult because my dad's a good man. Everybody knows that. But she left him all the same.

For as long as I can remember they've called me dad's girl. Always holding his hand, never far away. I heard it so often I believed it. Everywhere. Back home and out here. It was always the same. Only now I'm not so sure I am. I just might be my mother's girl, after all.

My mum, the slag who left a good man. And left her daughter. And a good home. They never said it like that, my dad's friends, but I could see it in their eyes, their grunts and their shuffling silences every time someone dropped the clanger of my mum's name. So, in time, I became dad's girl. But, deep down, I wasn't. And I'm sure if you sliced my dad open, you'd find another dad inside. The dad that got left. The dad that hasn't changed since he got left, that fossil deep inside.

Listen, I'm saying to myself. That's the voice you'll hear from now on. That's the other voice in your life.

And it's a good voice. But is it the voice I've been waiting all these years to hear? My dad thinks the worst thing that can happen to you is to be left. I'm not so sure. To be left, somebody's got to do the leaving. And that's a different story altogether. My mum was nineteen when she married my dad and he was twenty-one. Now, I'm twenty-one.

And I know I could just ignore this voice inside me and just go on with it all. This whole thing. I could. Allan proposed and I found myself saying yes. But I wasn't so sure then, and I'm not so sure now. And I think that's why I went through with it all. I went through with it hoping that that feeling, the one that tells you that you're sure about things after all, hoping that feeling would just come with the night and all my doubts would vanish in a puff of candle smoke. But they haven't and I've never felt more like my mother's girl in all my life.

And I know it sounds like a horrible thing to say, but if all this is true, if I'm her, if she's me, then I know why my mum left my dad.

39.

The Laugh

The first thing I hear when all the applause dies down is the laugh. I loved that laugh when I first heard it. From the moment I heard it. He gave that laugh everything he had. It was a big laugh. And he wasn't laughing at anyone. It wasn't a snigger, or a sly smile, or a sort of snort like Bruchner's got. It was big and generous. The sort of laugh you wanted to be around. You couldn't match it, but you wanted to join in with it, even if you didn't know what you were laughing at.

So, the first thing I hear is the laugh. And it strikes me that it's different. Something's gone out of it. It's not the same. It's loud, but it's not big any more.

He's talking to George Bedser. They laugh again. Bedser moves on. Vic always finds someone to talk to when he wants. You can be anywhere. A small town, and he'll bump into someone. Wait, he'll say on some platform in the middle of woop-woop, I've just seen a mate. But Bedser's moved away and Vic's eyeing me off because he knows what I'm going to say.

He's already got the slouch of a drinker. The body starts to wilt from the shoulders down to the feet, and the feet are last to go. You can see it passing through them, all of them. Like wax on a hot day, they just melt into the floor. The whole bloody lot of them. Vic's not there yet, but he's on the way. I can see that. And when he looks up I can see his eyes are getting that lost look. The question is do I tell him? Can I really be bothered? And should I tell him something's gone from his laugh while I'm at it? Should I tell him that when I hear it now I don't want to join in? That when I hear it now I know it's not the laugh it used to be. And instead of joining in, I just want him to please, please stop. To just shut up. I wish he could hear that laugh the way I hear it now and stop. Just like I wish he'd take it easy on the grog. So I'm walking across the floor wondering whether to tell him all this, and he's looking at me like he already knows what I'm going to say.

But if I say it I'm a nag. And who wants to be a nag? Everybody else's wife can be a nag, but not me. I'll never let anybody drag me down to that. I'll leave before I nag. And that's a promise. So we stand there beside each other, like strangers on a dance floor. And that might be fine, because we were strangers on a dance floor once and that was fun. Except then, we had it all in front of us. Silence then fed the anticipation. Silence was fun. But it's not fun any more. Because it's not that awkward silence that comes just before your life takes off like a rocket ship to Mars. Not that silence that comes just before all the nervous talk, when you blurt out all the things you've ever wanted to say because you've finally met someone you can say them to. No, it's not that kind of silence. It's just the familiar silence that comes after you've finally said it all.

So when the speeches start up again, it's a relief. We can stand beside each other in silence because we're listening to the speeches. We can stand beside each other and laugh because we're laughing at the jokes. And I'll hear that laugh and I'll know all over again that it's not the laugh it used to be.

40.

The Last of Vera

Rita and Vic are standing side by side while a family friend is telling Patsy Bedser's life story. The speaker leaves out the difficult events in their lives. He merely alludes to them. But this is enough to send a small flutter across George Bedser's sleepy eyelids. Embarrassing moments are being dragged out onto the public stage. There is laughter. Somebody is hooting. Patsy Bedser is looking away. George Bedser hears it all. He hears the happy sounds of his daughter's engagement, but he is not really listening.

It happened just the way you hear. I came home and she wasn't there. Not that she should have been, but I knew something was wrong. Straight away I noticed that. I don't know why, but there was a silence in the house like someone had stepped out for a bit longer than it takes to do the shopping. Or drop in on a movie. Or a friend. I know that kind of silence. There's a teacup on the sink, a half-eaten biscuit still resting on the saucer. And you know she's ducked out and she'll be back soon.

But it wasn't like that. The kitchen sink was clean. Bloody sparkling. And there were no messy cups around. No biscuits. No cakes. Everything was stacked away in cupboards like it is before a holiday. Like when we go to Blackpool every June for two weeks to see her parents. But it wasn't June and we weren't going on holidays. So I wandered through a spotless house. Vera always kept a clean house, but not like that.

Then, and I don't know why, I opened the drawers in the bedroom and her things were missing. So I opened another drawer, and except for a few odds and ends, they were all empty. Then I saw some old scarves hanging from the bedroom mirror, and her hats still on the rack in the hall, and I thought that maybe, maybe, it was all right after all. But I knew it wasn't. I knew it was all wrong.

I sat on the bed with my hat in my hands and I still hadn't taken my coat off. I didn't know how long I'd been home. Our Patsy was at her friend's like she always was after school and I was sitting on the bed staring at the empty drawers in front of me 'cause I hadn't shut them yet. Her lipsticks and powders and polish had gone from the dresser, but there was perfume in the air. It was fresh. I mean, it was really fresh. She could still have been standing by the mirror and I could have just been sitting on the bed tying my shoelaces and we could have been getting ready to go out. But I knew we wouldn't be going out anywhere again. So I closed my eyes and breathed it all in. The last of Vera.

I know that perfume. I'd know it anywhere. It's common enough, I suppose. But, even now, on the train or inside a shop. Even now I sometimes smell it, and think of Vera. I do. I was on the bed breathing her perfume in and thinking about getting up and following it about the house, like following her last steps, wondering where they'd end up, only I knew they'd end at the front door. I was sitting on the bed, the drawers opened and empty in front of me, the dresser cleared and bare, the smell of the perfume swirling round inside my brain, and I realised I was sitting on something.

I knew it was a bloody awful thing from the moment I picked it up. I saw my name on the envelope and I could tell it was Vera's hand that wrote it. She was always leaving notes around. Gone here, gone there. Back soon. I liked her notes. I'd always liked her notes, but I knew the one I was holding was a bloody awful thing before I even opened it.

It wasn't sealed and there wasn't much to it anyway. It started off Dear George, and that's as good as it got. Things aren't right any more, she said. Things hadn't been right for a long time, apparently. And she went on about things not being right and all for a bit, and I didn't have a clue what she was talking about. I brought the money home, didn't I? I didn't piss it up against the wall like some others. In fact, I wasn't one for going out much at all because I'd always rather be in with Vera and our Patsy. And that's God's truth. Not that I care about God. And I didn't boss her about like some others because I learnt very early on that you don't boss Vera. So I was looking at the letter trying to understand what she meant when she said things weren't right, but I couldn't figure it.

Then she talked about fun. I'm a good man, she said. She knows I'm a good man. And she made it sound like some kind of, some kind of limitation. Like I haven't got the imagination to be anything else. And that's when she said that she wasn't having fun. Not that it's my fault, she said. It was nobody's fault. But I'd no sooner than read it and I was thinking of all the fun we had the Friday before. Friday was the big night in our house. Always was.

And it was usually chips and fish in batter, a bit too much brown ale and soft drink for our Patsy. With a few of the old records and a bit of dancing before the old legs went funny. But apparently Vera wasn't having fun and that's why she'd decided to leave. Although, she never said she'd left. Not in the letter. It's not like the movies where the notes always say Dear somebody or other I'm leaving you. The fact was she had left because I could see all her clothes were gone. She didn't need to say it. I could see it all plain as the writing on the piece of paper in front of me and I was wondering what I was gonna tell Patsy when she walked in the door. That her mother'd gone because she wanted some fun in her life. Fun she called it.

At first I thought somebody was shaking me by the shoulders, the way people shake you by the shoulders when they're saying to you it's all right, you'll pull through, cheer up George. But nobody was there. Then I realised I was shaking all over and I can't even remember now if I ever finished that letter or not.

I learnt a week later that she took off with some flashy type. Some flashy type who sold things door to door. One of those shiftless flashy types that moves around the country, from place to place, and talks himself up because nobody else will. Because that's all he's got anyway. Talk.

And that's fun, eh? No home, no proper roof over your head. Just an old car filled with the useless junk that nobody in their right mind buys anyway, a flashy type in a cheap suit, and long days spent travelling from one town to another that looks more or less the same as the one you've just left. And that's fun? Well, it shows there's different types of fun in the world. And different types of people, who just might call that fun. But I don't call that fun. I call that bloody stupid. I did then, and I do now. Bloody stupid.

I don't remember what happened to that letter. I only remember breathing in Vera's perfume like she was still there in the house, and I remember getting up and walking about the house and opening all the windows.

When George Bedser finds himself suddenly looking round at the record player because there's a song playing, he realises that he must have missed the last of the speeches. Patsy is already slicing up pieces of engagement cake. Her fiancé is finding chairs for those who need them. Rita drifts out to the front lawn again, Vic stays in the hallway near the refrigerator. George Bedser's English friends are singing along to the record. Couples are dancing. George Bedser sits down. The party doesn't need him any more.

* * *

Minutes later, Patsy is standing on the porch farewelling the first of the guests to leave. The Millers, clutching their wrapped slices of engagement cake, wave from the street and begin walking back to their house. Doug Miller is not a drinker, but he is feeling light-headed as he lowers his hand after waving farewell, rests it on his son's shoulder and gazes up at the sky for the comet. This time next week, he thinks, he is scheduled to work late at the factory and will miss Saturday night with the family. But that's no matter. It is still a week away. And he doesn't really mind. Besides, he'll be finished by nine, the drive back from the factory is a short one, and he will be home for a late dinner.

The children are tired, their feet dragging. He carries his son, his wife carries their daughter. Behind them music from George Bedser's party is still audible and Doug Miller walks slowly back, whistling quietly along with the music, tired, but alive to every moment, every sight, every sound, every smell.

41.

Diesel and Steam

*A writer has said that the next best thing to
presence of mind is absence of body; and no doubt
many a driver would dearly have loved to be absent
in body in preference to facing some of the sudden
difficulties that have presented themselves.*

Bagley's Australian Locomotive Engine Drivers'
Guide

In the sealed world of the engine cabin Paddy
Ryan is leaning back in his seat. The diesel is
working without effort, the noise in the cabin is
minimal and the ride is a smooth one. Paddy is
alone. The fireman is still in the nose of the engine
preparing the tea.

The converging headlights part the darkness in front of him. The long, straight stretch of track that leads into the town at which they will stop for five minutes is visible for miles. Paddy is leaning back in his seat, eyes on the track before him. He is perfectly still. A study in concentration. A driver utterly absorbed in the job at hand; eyeing the track, glancing at the gauges before him, watching for the signals up ahead. But Paddy sees none of this. Paddy Ryan is dead.

He has just had a massive heart attack. It was all over in a second. Possibly two, but not likely. No time to call out. No time for any last words, if only muttered to himself. One moment he was leaning forward slightly, anticipating a mug of tea and licking the last of the ham and mustard from a troublesome tooth at the back of his mouth. The next his body convulsed and the bulk of Paddy Ryan fell back against his seat. His right hand, the hand that dwarfed so many pot glasses of beer, is firmly wrapped about the throttle.

Paddy Ryan, Queen's driver, Big Wheel driver, Loco's best, has quietly, and alone, passed from his working life into railway history. At his funeral, a week from now, the secretary of the union will deliver his eulogy, will say of Paddy that his kind will not be seen again, that nobody smoothed the rails like Paddy, that Paddy was the master of the smooth ride, and the master is gone.

The *Spirit* is travelling at just over seventy miles an hour and has just passed through the first of its red lights. The fireman is crouched in the nose of the engine, at its tip. He has unscrewed the top from the tea jar and is whistling quietly to himself as he shakes the tea leaves into the boiled water of the pot. He continues whistling to himself as the leaves sink into the water. He waits for the tea to brew before giving it a gentle stir. If they were not driving a diesel, if it were steam, the fireman would be sitting beside Paddy for there would be no nose to disappear into. The fireman would see what has happened and take over the train. But he can neither see nor hear the cabin from here. This is the young man's first job. He is nineteen. No wife. No girlfriend. The train has now passed its second red light.

Above him Paddy is still leaning back in the driver's seat, his dead eyes focused on the job in front of him. Paddy is unmoved as he passes through the red light, the light that tells him to slow and allow time for the goods to slip into the loop. Paddy is also unmoved when a pair of headlights sweep round a long bend in the track two miles away as the goods becomes visible for the first time.

The *Spirit* is still travelling at just over seventy miles an hour and the mile that it takes for the two engines to meet will be covered in less than a minute. The fireman is still crouched in the nose of the *Sir Thomas Mitchell* as the headlights of the two engines converge. Paddy remains unmoved, as if still concentrating on dislodging from his tooth that last, stringy strand of mustard-flavoured ham.

42.

Dancing with Evie

So I'm dancing with Evie, and I don't know how this happened, but it has. Rita left for the front lawn after the speeches, for a bit of air she said. Are you coming? No, I said. I'll stay for a bit. So she goes, and I stay put. Then Evie appears, a beer in her hand, and she's trying to get me to go outside because Rita's out there by herself. But I'm not budging. And she says she's not budging. So we settle in. And start talking. And all the time we're knocking back the beers. And she's no slouch with a beer, this Evie. And then somehow, somewhere along the way the talk stops, and we haven't got our glasses in our hands any more, we've got each other.

So, there I am. I'm dancing with Evie. And she's a beautiful dancer, Evie. I haven't danced in years and here I am dancing with her. She's beautiful at it. She's built like a dancer, too. And because I haven't danced in so long I've forgotten how you get the feel of a woman when you're dancing with her. Especially if she's built for dancing, like Evie is.

Did she ask me to dance? Did I ask her? Did we just start? I don't know, but we're dancing at the back of George Bedser's hallway near the kitchen. Everybody else is standing round after the speeches and there's a quiet song playing, and I know it so well but I'm buggered if I know where from. And all the steps are coming so easily, we seem to be gliding over this linoleum floor like it was marble. And I don't know if it's my imagination or the grog or what, but I could swear she's snuggling up to me. The way you do when you're dancing. Whatever, I'm bloody sure I can feel a whole lot more of Evie Doyle than I could at the start of the dance.

That's when I start singing. And I'm surprising myself because I'm remembering all the words, they're coming so easily, even if I still can't remember where I know the song from. It's got me buggered because I like to connect a song to a place or a time or a memory, because a song's not a song without a little bit of your life wrapped around it. So I'm singing away while we're dancing. Well, sort of whispering really. And she's a funny one, this Evie. She never calls me Vic, Victor or anything like that.

She calls me handsome. Always has. And I like the sound of it, even if it makes me laugh. Neither of us are saying anything at the moment because I'm still singing while we're shuffling round in small circles across that linoleum floor, with a bit of a breeze coming in from the back door. And just when I'm humming the piano solo, just when I'm about to start singing again, that's when I feel her hands go up around my neck, like she's supporting herself, or tired, or something.

It's automatic. The action pulls my head down towards her and I'm singing right in her ear. But soft. So only the two of us can hear. Besides, everybody else is standing round in the lounge room waiting for their cake. I can see the faint, light veins along her ear, I can see where it's been pierced, and I can see the colours of the stone earring hanging from it. And there's the perfume, and just below the perfume, I swear I can smell Evie's skin. And all the time I'm singing I can see how clear that skin is. Almost transparent. And warm too. I can feel the warmth coming off her. I'm singing in her ear so close I could almost kiss it. And then I do.

I close my eyes and don't ask me why or how, but I know she's closed hers too. I know this as surely as I know the song's finished, we've stopped dancing, and we're both standing perfectly still on the linoleum floor at the back of George Bedser's hallway.

I tell you, my eyes are only closed for a second. When I open them again Rita's standing by the kitchen door staring at us both and straight away I know I'm in a bit of shit. Evie looks around and she's gone without a word. Suddenly, it's just me and Rita. And I know, I know at that particular moment, I shouldn't be thinking any of this. But I can still feel Evie pressed up against me, like she's left dints in me or something. I'm standing there, trying to think of something to say to Rita, but all the time I'm whimpering inside like Bruchner's dog after he's waved a steak under its nose.

But before I can say a word. Before I can tell her it was an accident, that it was the grog, that it was just one of those things. That it was nothing. Before I can say any of this, she's off. It's all a bit confusing. One minute I'm dancing with Evie. Then Rita's at the door and Evie disappears without a word and I'm left standing in the hallway staring at Rita who shoots through before I get a chance to open my mouth. And to make things worse this crazy song starts up on the record player, and I'm listening to some young bloke with a bad case of hiccups. And everything seems louder. And when I step out from the hallway into the lounge room it looks like everything's gone slightly mad too. Because everyone's cleared a space and Patsy Bedser is dancing with some flash-looking type in the middle of the room. What's more nobody seems to quite know what's going on because Patsy Bedser's not dancing with the bloke she's just got engaged to. And it's obvious to me, and it's obvious to everyone else in the room that, whoever he is, they've danced together before.

But that's their business. I've still got the scent of Evie on me somewhere, Rita's just disappeared out the front door, giving it a good slap as she goes, and things have got themselves a bit tricky. But there's nothing else for it. I know she's at the front gate giving me two seconds to catch up. So I slide by the two dancers, which isn't easy because they seem to be all over the room at once, and call out good night to George over the music. Thanks for the party, I say, but George's not listening. And he doesn't see me wave because he's looking down at the floor.

It's only when I hit the warm, fresh air on the front porch that I realise I'm drunk. And it takes me by surprise. So I stand there for a moment just to steady myself. Bruchner, and Younger and Younger's wife are all standing in a small group on the lawn beside me. I'd give them a wave but I can't see the point because all I can hear is Bruchner's voice.

When I hit the street and look up to see Rita well in front of me and Michael on the other side of the street like he senses fireworks, I can't believe it's the same street we walked down just a few hours before. The sky's dark. I can barely see the long grass of the vacant lot next door to Bedser's and I can just make out the figure of Rita up in front of me. And even though I can't see it, I picture that dress of hers with the one strap and remember how keen she was to wear it tonight, and I know I've made a balls-up of things again.

43.

Steam and Diesel

*... what is a driver to do to ensure the safety of the
precious human freight whose faith in his abilities
never wavers? If he pulls himself together, fearlessly
does the right thing in the right way at the right
moment; if his judgement be quick as a flash, and
without hesitating he does the best thing to meet
the emergency, he shows himself in every way to be
the master of the situation, and lays indisputable
claim to be classed with the very best in his
profession.*

Bagley's Australian Locomotive Engine Drivers'
Guide

The first thing he sees when they round the bend is the *Spirit* coming straight at him. One look and he knows that train is really hammering. He also knows there is no point in applying the brakes because the *Spirit* shows no signs of slowing. The fireman and the driver quickly look at each other, and the driver tells the fireman to jump. The goods is still travelling at sixty miles an hour and the fall, at best, will be painful. Both men stand on the steps of their respective cabin doors, stare down at the passing ground, look quickly back at the approaching *Spirit*, and know there is only one course of action to follow.

But as the driver stares down into the blur of passing ballast on the side of the rails, he knows he won't jump. With one foot raised on the driver's side of the steps and both hands gripping the railings, he quickly looks back at the *Spirit* and tries to judge its speed. That diesel is hammering. That is all he can say with any certainty. But he knows his own engine. He knows what this thing can do because he's just let it off the lead and he knows it can move. It can move faster than any diesel on rails. What's more, he knows the loop is just up there. Within range, he's sure of that. And something tells him that it can be done. The engine can do it. It will get him there into the safety of the loop and the *Spirit* will then pass on as will the danger.

He also knows as he looks to the ground that his bones won't take the fall. He's sixty-four and his body is no longer capable of enduring a tumble like that, however happily he might land. In his own mind he can already see and hear his old bones shattering on impact with the ground like fallen glass. And there are the passengers on the *Spirit*, currently dozing in the night or sipping warm tea from their thermoses, oblivious of the situation. If a collision takes place at this speed people will die, he is certain of that. As his foot lands back on the cabin floor he knows what he must do. He knows that if he jumps now, and somehow lives, and if people die because nobody tried to stop the thing happening, he knows that the whole of his driving life will have been for nothing. All of this takes no more than a few seconds.

It is then that he turns round to the fireman. You jump, he can hear his voice calling out to the fireman, but calling from far away. I think I can make it, this voice is calling. And as soon as he utters those words, as soon as he calls them out into the speeding summer air, as soon as he hears his own voice calling from far away as if he were already a spectator to his own actions, as soon as he hears and notes all this, he knows he is about to die.

The fireman jumps. The driver is alone. Perhaps five or six seconds have elapsed since they first saw the *Spirit*. He knows what he must do. He rushes back into the cabin and immediately adjusts the speed. And, instantly, he feels the engine respond. He has faith in this engine and he is backing that faith now. As he stands at the window, staring straight at the approaching headlights and frantically calculating the distance between the *Spirit* and the loop, he is backing this engine to beat death. Diesel and steam. Steam and diesel. It's come to this.

44.

Bloody Michelangelo

Rita is well ahead of Vic, Michael is still on the other side of the street keeping his distance. The sky is black and the comet is a ball of flaming light in the sky. It's the first thing she sees when she finally turns, and she stands staring at it in the dirt street, with her cheeks still burning and her eyes still stinging. She knows she's as bright with the desire to live as that comet. It's big, and bold, and reckless, and she'd rather blaze across the sky for one summer only, than spend a lifetime of summers trailing after a drunken Vic and slowly dying. She runs her fingers down the soft, black material of her dress. She'll wear this dress again. But not in this backwater of a street where it's a crime to want to look good and everybody looks at you sideways if you try.

It's then she lowers her eyes to Vic plodding up the street, one of the tailor-made, cork-tipped cigarettes that he keeps for social outings in his mouth, and she rehearses what she'll tell him.

I've had you Vic. I've had enough. In fact, I'd had enough years ago. I just stuck around hoping things would get better, but they only got worse. So you can do what you like from now on. You can stuff your own life up all you like because I'm going. And why not? Everything has gone. The love, yes remember that? Well it's gone. You wore me down, Vic. And I never thought I'd live to say it, but it's gone. It's really gone.

But there's no point telling you now. You're too drunk to take it in. And even if you do, you won't remember in the morning anyway. I'll wait till you've slept it off. Till you're sitting down in the kitchen like you always do, staring down into your teacup with that bloody spoon going round and round. Then, I'll tell you. Vic, I'll say. Why couldn't you see it coming? Why? Because I've had enough for years now. I've had enough of spending my life trailing after some drunken bloody fool who imagines he's the bloody Michelangelo of engine driving. I've had it up to here. They're just bloody engines Vic. They're just bloody trains. And it's just a bloody job. But the whole thing, it all means more to you than I do, doesn't it Vic? It must. And that's why I'm going. That and the grog and the stupid bloody things you do just when we could have a good night. I'll tell you all that in the morning, Vic. But not before. I'd be wasting my breath.

Tonight there is nothing left to say and she turns away from Vic, away from the long, swaying grass of the paddock they'd all stood staring into only a few hours before, and she walks back towards the golf-course end of the street, the white gums growing bolder with every step.

45.

The Last Dance

From the gusts of laughter and the occasional clatter of applause, Jimmy can tell that the speeches have begun. Even from the car. And after an hour and a half of chain-smoking and listening to the radio, he has at last decided upon his moment. When the speeches are concluded and the applause has ceased, he will join the party, having specially selected from the stack of forty-fives beside him the record he will place on the hi-fi he sold to Patsy Bedser the previous autumn.

But for the moment he lights another cigarette and turns the radio up while the speeches continue. He drums his fingers on the steering wheel, while he looks around at the flat, square houses that are gradually beginning to fill the vacant spaces left over from the old farms. Music, like that which leaps from his car radio and from the hi-fi's of the shops. Music like that, once in a lifetime music, doesn't come from suburbs like these. Nothing comes from places like these. You must follow the music. You must follow it back into the speakers from which it comes. You must crawl back into the speakers, along the cables and wires along which it runs, to the hi-fi itself, to the arm and the needle, and spin with it all until the record finishes and the needle takes you back into the hole at its very centre, then you must disappear down that hole, like Alice, until you finally reach the source of it all. And once you are there, you will have arrived at the only place on earth that matters, because nothing matters more to Jimmy than the music that daily leaps into his life from the radio of his car and the hi-fi's of the shops that he visits. This music is calling him, and he is determined to follow it all the way back to its source. And when he is there he will be at the centre of things, at the centre of this sound. For, at the moment, he knows he is sitting at the extreme edge of it.

Light applause and cheers issue from the open windows of Patsy Bedser's house. Soft music begins and Jimmy knows that the speeches are over. He takes the record he has chosen from the top of the stack beside him, pushes the car door open, and steps out onto the dirt footpath. The car door creates a faint thud in the night as Jimmy closes it. He drops his cigarette on the footpath and begins the short walk to Patsy Bedser's front door.

At first nobody notices him. Or nobody cares. He's just walked in through the front door and he's standing in the lounge room with the record in his hand. He looks around the room, eyeing the faces for Patsy and noticing that he is beginning to attract a bit of attention because the guests are all realising that individually and collectively nobody seems to know who the young man is. He is, the relay of shrugging shoulders suggests, a stranger. But, of course, nobody is a stranger. And those of the party who are not dancing or deep in conversation, continue to stare at the young man either expecting him to explain himself or expecting the riddle of his presence in George Bedser's lounge room to be solved any second. And it is.

Patsy, he suddenly says. She's holding a tray of sliced cake and offering it to somebody in the corner of the room when she hears her name called. When she turns the first thing he notices is that her dress is all wrong. It makes her look like she's already been married a lifetime. Like she was always married. And all she can say when she turns and sees him is oh. And then, you? They've only spoken three words between them, but they've got the whole room in. Including George Bedser and the young man Patsy's just got herself engaged to.

Jimmy holds the record out to her. It's a present, he says. Congratulations. I hope I'm not intruding, he adds. But I was in the area and it seemed wrong not to congratulate you on such a special day. He's still holding out the record but Patsy Bedser hasn't accepted it because she's still staring at Jimmy like she's stumbled into a dream. And it's not hers. Take it, he says. It's an import. A first pressing. In fifty years it'll be a collector's item. Believe me.

And she does, because Jimmy knows his music. In the silence that follows, because the record on the hi-fi has just finished, she suddenly suggests they put it on. And when the music starts it is unlike anything that has been on the hi-fi that evening. It is a disturbance and the music confirms the unspoken suspicions of everybody in the room that this young man is trouble. And, aware that the whole room is watching, desperate to say something, to do anything but stand there and talk with the whole room straining forward to listen as this song pours out from the speakers into the room and then through the open windows and over the dark, swaying paddocks of the suburb, she suddenly curtsies before him as if inviting him to waltz, to dance. And then, suddenly, they are dancing.

That's when the room clears, creating a large space for the two of them in the centre of the lounge. Within seconds, Patsy and Jimmy are dancing like two well-rehearsed professionals. Like two people who are used to dancing with each other. This doesn't escape the party. Nor does it escape George Bedser who is now looking at the floor, wondering who on earth this young man is while knowing all along that he is trouble because he knows his type. He knows them already. He's seen them before. These slick, smooth poetic types that have no guarantee in them, like the shoddy goods they sell. And the more the music imposes itself on the party, seeming to render them all either obsolete or at the hour of their death, the more George Bedser wants to smash it.

But the dance continues and neither Bedser nor the puzzled young man who is her fiancé, can believe that the young woman dancing in the middle of the floor is their Patsy. And, of course, it isn't. It's another Patsy altogether, but they've only just discovered that.

And then, after a seemingly eternal two and a half minutes that bring with it a change so fundamental that the mood of the party is irrevocably altered, the music finally finishes and the dancing ends.

On the front porch a few moments later, Jimmy explains to Patsy that he's leaving the country. Her mind still turning round in circles as if she were still dancing, she asks where. And when he says Nashville she asks him again, convinced that she couldn't have heard right. But she did. He's going to Nashville because that's where the music comes from, and he wants to follow the music. He's tired of standing in hi-fi stores, listening to the most important thing that has ever happened in his life, from this impossible distance. He wants to climb into those speakers and follow the sound back along a pathway of connecting wires and leads, for as long as it takes, until he finally arrives at the source of it all. And that's why he's going to Nashville. He's no singer, he knows that. No performer. But, one day, perhaps, he just might be able to make those records whose music leaps out at him through the speakers of the hi-fi's he sells.

Then he's gone, with a wave and a kiss for luck blown through the air, his long legs crossing the street in easy strides, those cowboy lopes that she knows so well and is watching, she knows, for the last time. And as Jimmy's car passes, he waves again from the open window.

Broken-hearted melody . . .

She might have no desire to follow Jimmy, but she also knows now that she has no desire to return to the party. The soft, romantic music now playing on the hi-fi that Jimmy sold her is not her music, and the Patsy Bedser who, ten minutes before, was handing out slices of engagement cake to the guests, is now alien to her. And always was.

And so she sits, vaguely aware of the talk of her neighbours near her on the front lawn, and searches for the words she knows she will have to find.

46.

The Invitation

The first thing she does when she walks in the door is switch on the front porch light. It's an invitation.

The house is quiet the way an empty house is quiet and Evie takes a bottle of beer from the fridge and walks to the lounge room at the front of the house. There she switches the light on and sits with the venetians up so that the room is visible to the street. She knows that Rita must pass the house on the way back to hers, and so the house is open.

Her husband will be back in three days. He will stay for a week before he leaves again on another interstate trip. Normally, the empty quiet sound of the house doesn't bother her, but after the noise and music and confusion of the party it does.

Ten minutes before she was dancing with Vic, and as she leans her head back against the armchair she wishes it was one dance she'd never had. It was a foolhardy, stupid bloody thing, and God only knows how it happened. A bit too much grog, a bit too much time spent in an empty house. Who knows? But suddenly they weren't just dancing. And she wishes, more than anything, that she could have those ten minutes back again. And she would tell Rita all this. That it was a stupid thing, a stupid bloody little thing. But she can't have those few minutes back. They're gone. And she can now only tell Rita what she couldn't at the time. That it was just a nip. Just a peck. Does it need to matter all that much? But she knows it will. And as she sits contemplating all this she sees the figure of Rita step into view on the other side of the street.

But Rita doesn't turn. She acknowledges neither the house, the porch and lounge room of which are lit up and open to the street, nor does she acknowledge her friend, visible to her, sitting in her armchair and waiting for her to cross the street and join her so that she can explain it all. Rita turns her head away and walks the entire length of Evie's block facing the other side of the street as if the house and all its lights didn't exist.

And so Evie watches the only friend she's got in the street walk by. She lifts her beer, noting as she does, that there are two glasses on the tray beside her. Two glasses, like there always are, when Rita comes by on hot nights and they talk.

A few moments later Michael passes, staring down at his feet like he too has been forbidden to look upon the house of his mother's friend. Then Vic. And for a moment Evie could almost laugh. Ten minutes ago he was the smoothest, the most elegant of dancers on the floor at George Bedser's house, now he is a rubber man, swaying from one side of the dirt footpath to the other as he plods on by.

When they've all passed she switches off the porch light and sits back in the lounge room with only the dull glow of the reading lamp. She could write a note, she could post a letter, but she knows it wouldn't make any difference.

Outside, in the street, she can hear the scattered sounds of families making their way back from the party. There are calls of good night, farewell and goodbye, the sounds of occasional laughter, the tooting of car horns, a line from a song, a whistled tune left lingering in the night air. All along the street she can hear the sounds of the party breaking up. But inside, the house is quiet, the way an empty house is quiet.

47.

The View from the Schoolyard Pines

They began the night, the three of them, walking down the street together. Now they are scattered on separate sides of the road, the sounds of the party becoming more and more faint. Michael sees his mother ahead, his father following, back near Bedser's. But they are shadowy figures in the dimly lit street.

It's always like this. They're always leaving somewhere suddenly; a weekend visit to a country town, a railway picnic, a quiet drink at friends. Something always goes wrong and they're suddenly leaving, putting their coats on, grabbing their bags. Like tonight.

At the beginning of the night everything was as it should be. They were walking to the party together, like all the other families, and Michael was aware as they walked along the street that all nights should be like this. But they never are. Something always goes wrong and they wind up out in the street feeling their way back home in the dark.

Michael doesn't know what happened, what it was that caused them all to suddenly leave, but because his mother had deliberately looked the other way when she passed the lighted house of her friend, he concludes that he too should ignore the woman, and he senses that somewhere inside that house is to be found the cause of their sudden departure. So when he passes the house he looks down to the footpath, as if to look up, and nod or wave to the woman, like he would on any other night, would now be an act of betrayal. So he looks down until he is sure he has passed her house. When he does he checks behind him and sees the white-shirted figure of his father labouring home up the slight incline near the Bedsers'.

The night is over. And all the expectation they took with them at the beginning of the evening, as they walked along the street while the sky was still light with a golden peach glow, has come to this. All around him, the far-off sounds of the guests leaving, the bicycles left out on the lawns, a paper party hat dropped on the dirt footpath. All about him, everything has the look that things have when something is over. What they were at the beginning of the evening, what they had all looked forward to in their own private ways, has now become the past. And all the things that could have happened, all those things the night could have produced, all the possibilities it contained, have come to this.

Soon they will enter the house, one at a time. And when they do it will be filled with the familiar silence that comes to a house when nobody's talking. For a few moments, as they walked along the street earlier that evening, as they paused by the long grass of the vacant paddocks, the night seemed to contain the promise that things would be different. But it was never going to be different. Michael knows that. It was always going to end like this.

It is then that he stops, stock-still on the footpath with his hands clenched by his side and looks about the street, glowering into that warm, boozy Saturday night, demanding more of the world, with all the ridiculous rage and anger of a powerless child. To his right, swaying slightly above the houses, are the tall pines of the school. A row of five pines, tall as the mills. One Saturday morning he climbed the tallest of those pines. For a quarter of an hour, branch by branch, feet wedged into the gaps of the tree's trunk for grip, he climbed the tree.

Pausing on boughs as he did to regain his breath and strength in the hot summer air. But finally, he'd climbed as far as he could. There had been only a slight breeze on the ground, but the wind had been strong up there. He had gripped the branch that he sat on while the tree swayed from side to side. And sometimes, when the wind picked up, it almost seemed to topple forward as if it were about to fall over onto the playground, the shelter shed and the red school buildings of the third and fourth grade classes below him.

He's standing in the street looking at the pines, and he can feel the bark under his palms, smell the sap, and feel the cool wind on his face while he sways from side to side as if he were perched on the lookout of a ship's mast. And from those remembered, windy heights of the pine tree he can still see the suburb spread out below him as it was that morning; the dirt roads, intersecting and crossing each other in the morning sun, the old settlers' homes in the distance, the shining, silver railway lines that divide the suburb between east and west, the railway station, the flour mills beside the station, the factory owner's four acre mansion to the right of the mills, his Bentley parked at the end of a long, sweeping driveway, the grazing cattle on the shrunken farm in front of him, the bluestone farmhouse, the old stable, the old wheat road, the war memorial, the shops, the black, bitumen line of the main street, the golf course, the greens and fairways, the square, box houses with their bare yards and struggling gardens, and the dry creek that trickles through it all.

And almost directly below him, his own street. From up there he could see into everybody's yards, see old man Malek watering his potatoes, Mr Younger staring at a partially completed wall of his house with a hammer in his hand, Mrs Bruchner in her garden chair, and just coming into view, his father, turning off the main road and cycling towards their street after having finished the night shift.

He'd never seen it all so completely before, the street, the whole suburb, spread out below him. He had hurried down the tree, sliding down the trunk, stopping occasionally at the boughs and branches, until he dropped back onto the pine-needle ground and began running, determined to beat his father back home.

Suddenly, standing in the street, his fists clenched tight, his knuckles white and his nails biting into the soft flesh of his palms. Suddenly, he wants that view again. And instead of continuing along the street as he normally would, he turns and begins running down the small lane that leads to the creek. To his father he would only have been a faint blur of movement in the night, vaguely recognisable as his child. As Michael hits the creek he leaps it, lands with a thud on the other side, and continues running along the lane until he reaches the tall pines of the schoolyard. And, walking to the tallest of those pines, he begins to climb.

It is then, as Michael flies across in front of him, that Vic hears it. A low groan, coming from somewhere out beyond the flour mills, in the darkness of the paddocks where the suburb ends. He stands still and turns his ear to the sound, charting the car's course in his mind. Slowly, inexorably, the sound gathers in volume. He hears the gears changing, the car slowing, the wheels squealing, and he knows the corner that the car has reached and the road it is turning into.

Then the groan returns, more like a howl, and the long, uninterrupted run to the golf course end of the main road begins. From where Vic is standing he has a clear view through to the main road for there are no houses in front of him, only the open swaying grass of two vacant lots. As the car accelerates and the sound intensifies, shaking the whole suburb, Vic, to the exclusion of everything around him, concentrates on the view to the main street through the open section of the vacant paddocks. And then he sees it, a dark flash of gleaming black metal and shining chrome, low on the road and sleek. It is no sooner there than it is gone, accelerating into the night, into life, into death, towards the end of the suburb where the road runs out.

Hats are out of fashion. Vic no longer wears one. Nobody does any more. But had Vic been wearing one at that moment, he would have raised it.

The smell of the sap is stronger at night, the branches more difficult to find. But, slowly, step by step, Michael leaves the ground that is soft with pine needles below him, and branch by branch, climbs the tree. His eyes become keener the more he climbs, the moonlight stronger the higher he goes. The branches become surprisingly visible, the air cooler and sweeter, the climb a dream. And at the top, gripping the branch he is sitting on as it sways in the breeze that is always stronger at the top of the tree than at the base, he takes in gulps of cool, pine-scented air as if drinking water.

In the golf course to his right he sees the headlights of a car and he knows it's the police driving Hacker Paine home. His father told him that Mr Paine is still fighting the war. That he goes to the golf course and fights with shadows because his mind's not right and that his wife telephones the police and the police have to come and take him home every time.

Still gripping the gently swaying branch that he sits upon, he turns round towards the darkness of the schoolyard oval, the concrete cricket pitch invisible in the night. And as he does the thrill of the perfect ball passes through him, and he is sure that when he is ready, when he has taken in all that he can from the books that he keeps in his room, he will bowl that perfect ball and it will become known across the suburb as the ball that Michael bowled. And it will be agreed by all those who witness the event that the boy has a gift for speed. And it will be this, this gift for speed that he knows will one day carry him out of his street, out of his suburb, and into the world of the great Lindwall. For the kind of speed that turns heads can do all that. Calmly swaying on his branch at the top of the schoolyard pines, Michael waits for the day.

Below him, the lights of his street lead down to Bedser's. The house is still well lit, but he can just see people leaving, just hear the faint good nights, see the occasional car lights leaving the street and driving out into the darkness of the suburb.

He doesn't know it, but he has seen Patsy Bedser for the last time. She will leave the suburb the next morning, and the last image he will carry of her for years to come will be the Patsy Bedser who danced on her engagement night in her father's house with the stranger from the old country church. From the top of the pines he sees it all again vividly; the room is cleared, Patsy and this stranger are dancing. The music is loud and the dance is fast and exciting. This stranger twirls Patsy round and as she spins on the lounge-room floor she catches Michael's eye, laughs out loud like she did that afternoon he watched them at the old church, then taps his shoulder before continuing the dance. Of all the people in the room Patsy Bedser had chosen him to share the moment with, and he knew he should have waved or smiled or something. But he had suddenly looked to the floor and she had danced away. And once again, he was left wishing he could grow up fast. To dance with her, laugh with her, leave with her. When he finally looked up she was dancing on the other side of the room. Once more, out of reach.

But, most of all, as he concentrates on the dark rectangles he knows to be the vacant paddocks at which the family had paused earlier that evening, he sees, again and again, the three of them as they were, standing by the paddock with the evening before them. Three figures under a sky the colour of ripe peach. Again and again, as he watches from the top of the schoolyard pine, he sees them walk down the street to the party at Bedser's house, pausing by the paddock, breathing in the scents and the sounds of their suburb that for these few years will tremble between town and country. Once again, from the top of the schoolyard pine, he will watch as they walk down the unpaved, dirt road to Bedser's house at the bottom of the street. He will always watch them walking down the street to Bedser's house. He will always see them like this, and always at the same point in the walk. Again and again and again. And maybe, just once, in this endlessly repeated moment, a miracle will happen. And they will get it right, and things will be as they ought to be. Just once.

Epilogue

Sunday Morning

48.

The Bells

Before she even enters the kitchen she hears that bloody teaspoon, going round and round in the cup. And she knows when she opens the kitchen door she'll find him sitting there, staring down into his teacup, with that stupid, brooding look he gets on his face when he's made a mess of things. The one he keeps for Sunday mornings, the surly, whipped-dog look. She knows also that it will be a silent kitchen, and that the morning will be silent like all their Sunday mornings.

But none of that matters now. All their conversations, all their heart to hearts, all their attempts to talk a bit of sense into him came to nothing in the end. And this, she says to herself, this is the end. That's why she's leaving. Because there's no point staying when the show's over.

She can say all the things she rehearsed last night in the street walking back from Bedser's because now he's sober, now he can hear every word, and he won't have the excuse of being too drunk to remember what was said the night before. And that bloody spoon can go round and round in that bloody cup for an eternity because she'll never have to listen to it again. And, standing in the hallway, just as she is about to push the door open, she closes her eyes and pauses for a moment as she rehearses the words she could never once have imagined even thinking, let alone uttering.

He doesn't look up when the kitchen door opens, nor does he look up when Rita crosses the room and takes a cup down from the cupboard. He stops stirring his tea. The spoon stops going round and bloody round, and it's like the bells have ceased ringing in some giant cathedral. The radio becomes audible, but she doesn't listen to it. She is formulating in her mind what has to be said. The radio is a quiet, almost comforting sound, but it doesn't interrupt her thoughts. The words are ready. The time is right.

But it is only then that she suddenly understands why Vic has stopped stirring his tea. It is because he has turned towards the radio and the spoon is still only so that he can hear it better. He is not listening to a song, or music or an amusing story. It is the news. To the exclusion of every thing else, he is concentrating on the words that are being spoken. Rita forgets her prepared speech for the moment, and follows the line of Vic's eyes until she too is staring at the small plastic radio on the bench beside her.

It is not so much the words as the tone of their delivery that tells her something is wrong. An event from the previous night is being spoken of. A small town is mentioned, not far from where they lived soon after they married. Then two familiar names are listed, and with a silent, inward moan she knows beyond doubt that the people she attaches the names to are now dead. Then come the details. The number of the dead and the injured, the trains, the hour of the accident. And as she stares from the radio to Vic she knows, in an instant, that she will never utter the words she came into the kitchen to say. That in between formulating the words in her mind and being able to say them, this bloody awful thing has happened. And she knows, she knows beyond doubt, that Vic is a goner. So does he. One look and she can tell. One look, and she can read every single thing that's going through his mind. And it all comes to this. He's a goner. And when the music returns to the radio, instead of announcing that she's had enough, instead of saying that this is the end, that the show's over and that there's no point hanging about because you just wind up sitting around in the dark by yourself. Instead of saying all this, Rita crosses the floor and places her hand on Vic's shoulder.

The comforting gesture seems to go unnoticed because Vic shows no reaction. He is simply staring at the bare, white kitchen wall without blinking or moving any part of his face or body.

After an accident like this, Rita knows without being told, there will be an investigation. What happened, and why it happened, will need to be established. All the drivers will be examined, their medications scrutinised, and Vic won't stand a chance once all that starts. Not with the pills he takes, not with the turns he takes, on top of all the grog he puts away. You're finished Vic, she could say. You're finished with driving you poor bugger. What are you going to do now? What are we all going to do? For within a matter of minutes Rita has come to the inescapable conclusion that Vic is about to lose his job. It may take weeks, it may take months, but it will happen. And she knows, above all, that for all his whingeing and whining about the hours and the shifts and the mess and the dirt, that he'll be lost without his job. They'll offer him a desk, but you can't drive a desk, can you Vic?

And as soon as she recognises all of this, she also realises that it is an impossible time to leave him. That what she came to the kitchen to say will now have to be left unsaid. He will be lost. She will stay. And even as she recognises the inevitability of the situation, there is also a part of Rita that immediately knows that if she can't leave now, she never will.

In the bedroom, a few minutes later, she puts the small, cloth suitcase back on top of the wardrobe, then slumps back onto the bed and stares out the window at the dirt street, and the stirred dust of a hot, gusty Sunday morning.

There she forgets about what will now be left unsaid, and thinks about what might still be said. About the things that just might still be worth saying. About the things that might just be worth a go. Who knows, Vic, she could say. Who knows, you may have had the art of engines. But you don't have the art of simply living. The gift of just living. Of just being. Is this the one you've got to learn? Is this the one I've got to learn? Is this the one that's escaped us all these years? The simple, bloody art of just living your life. And not as if every day will be there like it was the day before, because one day it may not be. But as it should be. Just living every moment we're lucky enough to get, Vic, without all this looking back, and looking forward, and looking away. Do you think we can learn this one, Vic? Do you think we're up to it? Do you think we can? I hope so. I really hope so, because if we can't, we're not going to be much good to each other, or anyone else. We give all our energies to engines and trains and God knows what else, and we forget that we're alive. We forget that we're bloody well alive.

Vic is concentrating on the radio. He is aware of the fact that Rita is in the room. That she has touched his shoulder. That she has left the room. The radio is once again playing the soft, romantic music it always plays, the kitchen is quiet again, and Vic is left with the echoes of names, places, and times.

Paddy Ryan, Queen's driver, Big Wheel driver, the master artist of engine drivers, is gone. The classroom of his engine cabin, the master's studio where the young Vic learnt his trade, is gone too. Paddy Ryan has committed the most basic of blunders, and in such a way as to drag the whole of his driving career into disrepute. Until now the name of Paddy Ryan has been synonymous with everything that is the best. The very finest. But from now on his name will be synonymous with this. And all the years that went before will count for nothing. This will be Paddy Ryan's lasting legacy. Not his inexplicable gift for smoothing the rails, but his final shift. For, when it mattered, all his art, all his knowledge counted for nothing, and he committed the most basic of blunders. And it is for this that Paddy Ryan will be remembered.

It is not only Paddy's name, thinks Vic, but everybody's. They will all be investigated now. They will all be examined. And Vic knows he will lose his job. His dream of joining the Big Wheel is so close he can almost see his name on the roster board. But he knows now that it will never appear there, that the object of a lifetime's labour will not be his, that it will be suddenly taken from him at the very moment it seemed assured. Through the sheer slog of the years of driving, of pushing old engines beyond their capacity, of difficult shifts, of impossible weather and wasted hours in country stations waiting for the signal to proceed. Through all this it was the object of being rostered on the Big Wheel that kept him driving. If that were to be achieved it would all have been for something. He could relax then. He would have the best shifts, the best trains, the best engines. For his final years as a driver he would have it made. But not now.

And all because Paddy Ryan ran two sets of red lights. Vic knows the loop. He knows the procedure. He knows exactly what has to be done, as does any junior driver. And he slowly shakes his head at the incomprehensibility of it all. If Vic has ever had anything that could be called a faith, if he has ever believed in anything, if anything has sustained him and given him dignity through all these years, it is the art that he brought to his job. The art that they all did. The belief that something could be known so thoroughly, and performed so perfectly, that it became an art. But now the best, the very best, had blundered, just at that point in his career when he should have been invulnerable, and the faith that he embodied inviolable. But now, that faith is shattered.

Now, all of that is gone, and as he sips his tea he realises it is cold and he has no idea how long he's been sitting in the kitchen. Or when it was that Rita had entered the room and touched his shoulder. Or when it was that she had left the room and closed the door behind her.

The best had blundered. The faith of a lifetime has now been shattered. Paddy Ryan is gone. Finished. And so is the *Spirit* that he drove. They might put the thing back together, as if nothing had happened. And in time people will forget. But they can put it back together all they like. Vic knows that he'd rather bow out now, having lived through a time when he could have driven the *Spirit*, the true *Spirit*, rather than be the poor bastard who had to drive what was left of it.

Suddenly it starts, like giant bells tolling the end of an era. The spoon goes round and round and round, and soon the kitchen, then the house, is ringing with the sound.

ACKNOWLEDGEMENTS

Many thanks to the following organisations and people for their help during the writing of this novel:

The Australia Council for a Category B Fellowship granted in 1988.

The Musée de Pont-Aven, Brittany, France, for a two-month residency in October/November, 1998.

Laurie Clancy, Martin Flanagan, Gary Moorhead and Norm De Pomeroy (retired locomotive engine driver, Victorian Railways) for their editorial advice.

Shona Martyn, Linda Funnell, Rod Morrison and Vanessa Radnidge at HarperCollins, and my agent Sonia Land, for their support and enthusiasm.

Finally, my special thanks to Fiona Capp for her constant help, suggestions and advice during the writing of the book.

NICK HARKAWAY

The Gone-Away World

'Breathtakingly ambitious . . . A bubbling cosmic stew of a book, written with
such exuberant imagination that you are left breathless by its sheer ingenuity'
OBSERVER

The Jorgmund Pipe is the backbone of the world, and it's on
fire. Gonzo Lubitsch, professional hero and troubleshooter, is
hired to put it out – but there's more to the fire, and the Pipe
itself, than meets the eye. The job will take Gonzo and his best
friend, our narrator, back to their own beginnings and into
the dark heart of the Jorgmund Company itself.

Equal parts raucous adventure, comic odyssey and geek
nirvana, The Gone-Away World is a story of – among other things
– love and loss; of ninjas, pirates, politics; of curious heroism
in strange and dangerous places; and of a friendship stretched
beyond its limits. But it is also the story of a world, not unlike
our own, in desperate need of heroes – however unlikely they
may seem.

'Dazed and comic awesomeness'
GUARDIAN

'With his debut The Gone-Away World, Nick Harkaway has created
a fictional universe that is out of this world.'
TATLER

'[A] post-apocalyptic triumph . . . Immensely rewarding . . .
Genuinely terrifying'
THE TIMES

CRAIG SILVEY

Jasper Jones

Winner of the Indie Book of the Year Award 2009

Jasper Jones has come to my window. I don't know why, but he has. Maybe he's in trouble. Maybe he doesn't have anywhere else to go.

Late on a hot summer night at the tail end of 1965, Charlie Bucktin, a precocious and bookish boy of thirteen, is startled by a knock on his window. His visitor is Jasper Jones. Rebellious, mixed-race and solitary, Jasper is a distant figure of danger and intrigue for Charlie. So when Jasper begs for his help, Charlie eagerly steals into the night by his side, terribly afraid but desperate to impress.

Jasper takes him to his secret glade in the bush, and it is here that Charlie bears witness to a horrible discovery. In this simmering summer where everything changes, Charlie learns to discern the truth from the myth.

By turns heartbreaking, hilarious, tender and wise, *Jasper Jones* is a novel to treasure.

'Jasper Jones confronts inhumanity and racism, as the stories of Mark Twain and Harper Lee did ... Silvey's voice is distinctive: astute, witty, angry, understanding and self-assured.'
WEEKEND AUSTRALIAN

'Impossible to put down ... There's tension, injustice, young love, hypocrisy ... and, above all, the certainty that Silvey has planted himself in the landscape as one of our finest storytellers.'
AUSTRALIAN WOMEN'S WEEKLY

Lauren Groff

The Monsters of Templeton

Shortlisted for the Orange Broadband Award
for New Writers 2008

'The Monsters of Templeton *is everything a reader might have
expected from this gifted writer and more*'
STEPHEN KING

'*A vibrant patchwork of fact, fiction and myth . . . Beautifully rendered*'
DAILY MAIL

Willie Cooper arrives on the doorstep of her ancestral home
in Templeton, New York in the wake of a disastrous affair
with her much older, married archaeology professor. That
same day, the discovery of a prehistoric monster in the lake
brings a media frenzy to the quiet, picture-perfect town her
ancestors founded. Smarting from a broken heart, Willie then
learns that the story her mother had always told her about her
father has all been a lie. He wasn't the one-night stand Vi had
led her to imagine, but someone else entirely.

As Willie puts her archaeological skills to work digging for
the truth about her lineage, a chorus of voices from the town's
past rise up around her to tell their sides of the story. Dark
secrets come to light, past and present blur, old mysteries are
finally put to rest, and the surprising truth about more than
one monster is revealed.

'*A pleasurably surreal cross between* The Stone Diaries *and*
Kind Hearts and Coronets'
GUARDIAN

HILLARY JORDAN

Mudbound

Winner of the Bellwether Prize for Fiction

'*A page-turning read that conveys a serious message without preaching*'
OBSERVER

When Henry McAllan moves his city-bred wife, Laura, to a
cotton farm in the Mississippi Delta in 1946, she finds herself
in a place both foreign and frightening. Henry's love of rural
life is not shared by Laura, who struggles to raise their two
young children in an isolated shotgun shack under the eye of
her hateful, racist father-in-law. When it rains, the waters rise
up and swallow the bridge to town, stranding the family in a
sea of mud.

As the Second World War shudders to an end, two young men
return from Europe to help work the farm. Jamie McAllan is
everything his older brother Henry is not and is sensitive to
Laura's plight, but also haunted by his memories of combat.
Ronsel Jackson, eldest son of the black sharecroppers who live
on the farm, comes home from war with the shine of a hero,
only to face far more dangerous battles against the ingrained
bigotry of his own countrymen. These two unlikely friends
become players in a tragedy on the grandest scale.

'*This is storytelling at the height of its powers*'
BARBARA KINGSOLVER

'*Jordan builds the tension slowly and meticulously, so that when the
shocking denouement arrives, it is both inevitable and devastating …
A compelling tale*'
GLASGOW HERALD

STEVEN CARROLL

The Time We Have Taken

Winner of the 2008 Miles Franklin Literary Award

That exotic tribe was us. And the time we have taken, our moment.

1970, Glenroy. One summer's morning Rita is awakened by a dream of her husband, only to look out on an empty bed. It's been years since Vic moved north and left her life, but her house holds memories and part of her remains tied to a different time. As their son Michael enters the tender and challenging realm of first love, he too discovers that innocence can only be sustained for so long.

As they prepare to celebrate Glenroy's 100th anniversary, the residents of the Melbourne suburb look back on an era of radical change. The time has come for them to consider the real meaning of progress — both as a community and in their personal lives.

The Time We Have Taken is a powerful and poignant look at the extraordinary that lies within the ordinary, from a writer of breathtaking prose.

'*A writer worth cherishing. His prose is unfailingly assured, lyrical, poised.*'
AUSTRALIAN